TO: the Coopers — I am [illegible] to have such friends — and [illegible] you are the owners of "Pup-Pup's ol' place."

Dither Me Dead

Enjoy the flight. — Peace, Jim O

by

James W. Opalka

James W. Opalka

PUBLISH AMERICA

PublishAmerica
Baltimore

First printing

This book is fiction. The places, characters, names and events are the product of the author's imagination. Although Cape May, Cape May County Airport, The Hughes Technical Center, the banner-towing Cubs and the Southern Jersey Shore exist, the events and characters contained within this book are fictitious. They are used fictitiously and although certain regional locales are real, the events surrounding them and taking place therein are inventions of the author. Events surrounding the Cirrus SR-22 and all other aircraft are purely fictional.

ISBN: 1-4137-9871-3
PUBLISHED BY PUBLISHAMERICA, LLLP
www.publishamerica.com
Baltimore

Printed in the United States of America

To Paula, the one who helps the most, my life partner and soul mate, to whom I owe my life.
And to Weezie—my hero and teacher.

FACT FROM FICTION I

The United States Government, under order of the President, has instituted what is called Selective Availability (SA), a technique to reduce the accuracy of GPS (Global Positioning Systems) in the U.S. These devices are used primarily for aviation and nautical navigation.

The government did what is affectionately called "dithering," which is to say that satellite clocks used to transmit information to the GPS receivers were intentionally messed up. In other words, it put out incorrect information and created positional errors to anyone using the U.S.-based technology. The dithering was used to protect the security interests of the United States and its allies by denying access to adversaries.

By order of the President of the United States, the use of Selective Availability was discontinued on May 1, 2000.

It is also a fact that there are a group of homemade GPS hackers capable of emulating the dithering techniques used by the U.S. These GPS hackers can make their hacking devices from components obtained at any electronics supply house.

What is more disturbing is that experts believe the homemade jamming instruments will access more than the civil GPS signals, known as the C/A code, broadcast on 1575.42 MHz. They will also have the capability to seize control of the military frequency on 1227.6 MHz.

Not just aviation would be targeted. The Coast Guard operates GPS maritime navigation systems on both coasts, the Great Lakes, inland waterways and Hawaii.

What adds additional validity to this threat is that Transportation Secretary Norman Mineta ordered an action plan to protect civil GPS signal users by "the transferring of appropriate anti-jam technology from the military to civil use."

Many of the jamming methods and technological arts needed to attack the signals are available on the Internet. It would be naive to believe that no malicious attacker, no foreign adversary or psychotic techno-terrorist would use this catastrophic recipe for destruction.

Some of the questions that hang in the balance are obvious; others remain less predictable.

FACT FROM FICTION II
THE WILLIAM J. HUGHES TECHNICAL CENTER, ATLANTIC CITY, NEW JERSEY

The William J. Hughes Technical Center is, in fact, our nation's premiere aviation research and development center. The Federal Aviation Administration's (FAA) facility is located ten miles northwest of Atlantic City. It has succeeded in developing the most sophisticated and accurate satellite navigation system for instrument and visual flight use since the invention of the Global Positioning System. It has extended the parameters of usage to include extremely accurate vertical and horizontal guidance. It is accurate to within inches of a target.

WAAS (Wide Area Augmentation System) enhances the accuracy and reliability of Global Positioning Systems, specifically aircraft instrument landing systems.

Using recent improvements, the system opens pilot access to upwards of 500 satellite runway procedures at more than 200 U.S. airports. This accelerated 21st century technology will be used by virtually all commercial, business and private aircraft within the U.S.

However, WAAS will also make precision approaches available at literally thousands of airports that presently have no ground-based landing capability. The door is suddenly wide open in a new and much more intricate game of global terror.

PROLOGUE

The man in the blue leather recliner pushed pause on the remote. He sat in the darkened room staring at the body. He pulled the lever on the left side of the chair and watched his feet elevate. He lit a cigarette, holding it European style with his thumb and index finger.

"*Dzien dorby*," he said, *good morning,* looking at the body.

The corpse was inverted, hanging from a chain, naked except for an area of #10 mil three-inch duct tape wrapped around the circumference, covering the buttocks and genitals.

The format of the picture on the monitor was a dizzying fisheye view so as to take in an extreme wide angle. It distorted the image, made it look otherworldly, like falling off the edge of the earth.

"Troglodyte creep," the man said. "Son of a bitching Yahoo. You geek bastards all alike."

The body was painted white except for two red orbs coloring the eyelids like clown eyes. A tear, apparently painted before the body was inverted, flowed upward.

The man in the chair stood and raised his arms like a maestro, using his cigarette as a baton to direct a world-class symphony. He pointed at the monitor. Soft music played in the background.

"There's the problem," he said aloud, pointing at the inverted man.

There the bastard hangs...

"*Do widzenia*," he said. "Goodbye."

1

Two young men slid the cadaver gurney out of the ambulance. There was a rolling sound, metal on metal, as it trundled off stainless castors. The legs made a cracking noise as they snapped to their 90-degree position.

The driver held the gate leading to the ramp. The man who had been riding shotgun pushed the gurney. They headed toward a pilot standing by her plane.

Sunny Patronski had arrived at Cape May County Airport two hours early to fuel and preflight her Cirrus SR22 for a Lutherlyn Mercy Flight to Allegheny County Airport in Pittsburgh. She was waiting for a sick child and escort. She had volunteered to fly them to Pittsburgh for a procedure at Children's Hospital. She would remain there until the brief procedure was completed, then fly her passengers back home to Cape May.

She leaned against the leading edge of the right wing, her arms folded over her chest. She wore large aviator sunglasses and a light denim jumpsuit. Her hair was wet-look black and her face tanned from the ocean wind and sun. An oversized gold zipper extended from just above her crotch to the center of her chest, a tasteful amount of cleavage exposed. Within the cleavage a gold cross hung by a gold chain. Freckles, accentuated by the sun, dotted her chest. She had on lime-colored Adidas tennis shoes with black stripes. She was a handsome, athletic looking woman, beach-weathered and about 30 years old. The ambulance men enjoyed watching as they pushed the gurney.

She wondered why anyone would be rolling a corpse past her plane. There was nowhere for them to go beyond where she had the Cirrus tied down. There were only the crisscrossing runways of Cape May County with no other aircraft in sight.

"Gentlemen, what's this?" she asked. "Uh, I feel sort of silly asking, but is that a corpse you have in the bag?"

"Yes ma'am. Where you want it?"

"Preferably buried in a cemetery. Why do you ask?"

Before they could answer, a rusting Crown Victoria pulled in behind the ambulance. Dr. Carl Farnley, Cape May County Medical Examiner, struggled to get out.

At 50, Farnley's 300 pounds sagged disproportionately to his 150-pound frame. It was hard work for him to move.

He reached the plane gasping for air and dabbing at his face with a handkerchief, his powder-blue suit coat wet under the arms. Moisture dripped down his neck onto a blue oxford shirt with a blatantly discernable ring around the collar. He wore a bright yellow tie stained with breakfast or lunch residue. He hadn't had supper.

"Been waiting long, Sunny?"

"You look hungry, Carl," Sunny said. "By the way, don't bullshit me. Tell me this isn't my mercy flight. I mean, *mine* have always been alive."

"And alive it once was, neighbor. You fueled, ready for the Pittsburgh flight?"

Sunny stood in front of Farnley, looked down at her feet, shook her head and took off the aviator frame, Ray-Bans. She bent over and picked up a piece of limestone and threw it into the grass just beyond the airport Cyclone fence.

"Don't neighbor me, Carl. Just because we are, doesn't mean I'll fly corpses for you. You said it was a kid and escort. You lied."

"I need this guy in Pittsburgh tonight. It's important."

"Oh, I see. That justifies lying. I'll be alone with this carcass in pitch blackness over the Alleghenies."

"Don't say carcass. You will be flying the *remains* of Clayton Meadows. Not a carcass. Listen, this will help. The ancients had what they called mellified man. It was steeped in honey. These advanced people had human dumplings, Sunny. I shit you not. Dumplings, for God's sake. I'm not asking you to eat it. Just fly the son of a bitch to Pittsburgh, come home and we'll do dinner. You fly, I'll buy."

"A body bag? Really, Carl. You think your factoids help?"

The hot air was heavy and no wind moved in from the ocean to cool the oppressive evening. Sunny put up the collar of her denim jumpsuit and dabbed the moisture on her neck. She folded the collar back down and flattened it neatly.

"Correction," he said. "This is not a body bag. And corpses have needs, too. You have to have respect."

Farnley grabbed a piece of the bag, up where the head appeared to be. He rubbed his index finger and thumb over the material as though inspecting fine silk from the orient.

"Excellent," he said. "That's no six-dollar-and-fifty-cent chicken-shit bag."

Sunny's mind went to the lines of perspiration streaming down the small of her back.

"It's a crime scene disaster recovery bag with a numbered lock," Farnley said. "Envelope postmortem bags like this don't come cheap. Nothing but the best for you, Sunny. I'm telling you, the guy's locked in there and he ain't goin' nowhere fast, baby."

"Wrap him in aluminum foil for all I care. He is dead. This is creepy. I feel funny. I can't help it."

Farnley put his hands together, praying to her. "Do this one for me, *please*," he said. "Anything you want. We'll do the Sloshingburger on the beach."

"You'll spring for The Breakers Inn or Hearthside Bay. You can keep your lousy hamburger," Sunny said.

The ambulance guys looked at the couple and snickered, unsure whether the debate was humorous or tragic. They'd heard numerous disagreements between the two, usually good-natured debates. But one could never tell. Farnley grabbed the gurney and jerked it to stop the EMTs from taking Meadows back to the ambulance.

"Hell's fire, girl. This is truly a non-event. Like I said, in Arabia they used to have what they called mellified man, a human confection. Probably tasted like chicken."

"You're a sick puppy, Carl."

"Sunny, let me tell you. Speaking of chickens, the head of a stiff, excuse the expression, is about the size of a chicken and weighs roughly the same. Think of it like that. It'll help you through this. You know, whatever gets you through the night flight."

Farnley gently cradled the head of the corpse in the bag. He lifted his hands, showing the measurement, like he was holding a soccer ball. He bent down and kissed it.

"What'd I tell you?" he said. "Chicken-size. Pawk pawk."

Sunny pointed at his tie. Farnley looked down at the splotches. He spit into the palm of his hand and rubbed at the smears. He talked while he rubbed.

"I can't hire anyone for this. I'm over budget now. What's one dead one every once in awhile? I mean, come on, we're neighbors and friends. Aren't we?"

Sunny stood looking at the gurney and the body in the bag as though it was going to do something to make her decision easier. Maybe there would be a movement or gesture indicating the corpse was benign, a thumbs-up from Meadows, a good-guy cadaver, as opposed to some repulsive, malignant stiff. Corpse personalities.

She considered including the contents of the bag when calling in her flight plan to Atlantic City Flight Service Station. The operative phrase when submitting a flight plan was, How many souls on board? Dead or living?

"Come with me, Carl. Take care of the package. Keep me company. I'll fly. I'll buy."

"Are you kidding?" he said. "I don't fly. I take trains, not planes."

Her stomach knotted, and she didn't like the images painting in her head. They became colorful, dramatic. The perspiration increased, streaking to her buttocks and she thought about her makeup and then about how petty it was and maybe she'd never put makeup on again; maybe never talk to her medical examiner neighbor again.

"Nothing will rub off if you touch it," Farnley said. "The guy is no afterlife cootie carrier. There's no germ of dread that's gonna burrow inside you, wait for the perfect time, then transform like in some kind of creepy movie. That's bullshit. This is science here. Besides, that bag is the best. Hell, Sunny, they even use plastination as artwork in some parts of the world. It's a technique of tissue preservation. Keeps everything normal size. This scientist in Germany takes and—"

"Carl, don't go there. I don't want to know."

"Art, Sunny, it passes off as art to some people."

"Tell me how to ignore this thing the entire flight to Pittsburgh, Carl? Also, tell me, do you smell paint, or is it just me?"

"Oh, I smell you, Sunny. And you are delicious."

"Stop it, Carl."

"It's nothing, Sunny. I couldn't get it all off."

"Carl, you don't paint. I've never seen you with a brush in your hand at Maycomb Beach Condos. And that's not paint on your tie, probably more like hamburger grease, maybe bacon."

Farnley pointed to the corpse. "I couldn't get all of it off Meadows," he said. "Pittsburgh forensics will be pissed, I know. But what the hell? It's a medical solvent. It'll dissipate. He's fresh."

She waved her hand at Farnley and made a face like she was a little girl taking horribly distasteful medicine and if she swallowed quickly it wouldn't be so bad. She motioned to the ambulance crew to put the body in her plane.

Besides, she thought, *Allegheny County isn't that far away at 200 miles an hour. And it is speechless cargo, zipped and locked in a crime scene disaster recovery bag, envelope postmortem container with a numbered lock. What trouble could he possibly make?*

2

The pilot of the Cessna Citation turned west and began a standard instrument departure from Atlantic City International Airport. Matt Harmond reached into the leather pocket beside him, fingered through some magazines and opened up *Newsweek*.

He put it down a minute later and looked up at the pilot and copilot going through their checklists preparing for the climb to a cruising altitude of 35,000 feet. Harmond watched the red flickering display on the bulkhead behind the pilot light up to indicate the Citation's speed at 340 knots.

Beside the knot indicator, the LED readout interpolated the airspeed at 391 miles per hour. The colorful lighting was supposed to be for the enjoyment and distraction of tired passengers. Matt Harmond wasn't enjoying it and certainly was distracted.

He tore off the cover of *Newsweek* and threw it at the pilot. "Where are we?" he said. "We there yet, Butch?"

The pilot took his headset off and turned to Harmond. "Well, Mr. Harmond, I'm not exactly sure where we are, sir, but we're really going like hell."

Butch Dominion looked over at his copilot, motioned him to take the controls and pointed to a heading on the gyrocompass to follow. He bent over, picked up the crumpled magazine cover and stowed it in his flight bag.

Dominion, chief pilot for Flight Control International, was a meticulous man, especially when it came to flying. He was precise in his cockpit resource management and thorough in his procedures.

He learned to fly when he was in high school. He washed planes, swept and cleaned out hangars and cut grass at the Brandy Star Airport in West Chester County, Pennsylvania, not far from the famed home of artist Andrew Wyeth.

He'd get an hour of flight instruction after a lot of work hours. He worked for every single moment of instruction he received, and as a result became obsessive in his flying habits. Two hundred and forty degrees meant exactly that. Thirty-five thousand feet had to be exactly that. Butch Dominion permitted himself no room for error.

The FAA knew it and liked it, so when Federal Aviation Administration pilots were otherwise occupied, the FAA's William J. Hughes Technical Center in Atlantic City gladly hired FCI and its chief pilot to deal with the agency's transport needs.

Matt Harmond knew Dominion was not a fly-by-the-seat-of-your-pants pilot. So when Matt jokingly asked a second time where they really were and Dominion indicated with a shrug of his shoulders that he wasn't exactly certain, Matt undid his safety belt and moved up to the front office of the speeding jet.

"We're supposedly one of the lucky ones, Mr. Harmond. We have the WAAS installed, your new Wide Area Augmentation System. You guys even put it in. We also have the LAAS, your Local Area Augment System. Best of both worlds. But I'm looking at the indicators and everything is saying I'm headed to Cleveland. Now, this is pretty basic geography, navigation 101 stuff. And if I'm not mistaken, everything is telling me to turn north to pick up my on-course heading. Now, dead reckoning navigation, again real basic stuff, tells me if I do that, I'm going to get us to Toronto real fast, and you won't be seeing Cleveland till we circumnavigate the earth. Clear day like this, not a cloud in the sky. Any student pilot or elementary geography student can see that."

"Can't be," Harmond said. "I put this thing together and it's ready to be distributed to just about every air carrier in the U.S. The thing is supposed to be dead balls on the money, Butch. It cannot be off."

"This isn't the first time, Mr. Harmond."

Harmond shrugged his shoulders and threw up his hands in disgust. He'd been working for the Technical Center ever since the inception of the WAAS and LAAS projects.

The satellite-enhanced en-route and landing system had been his life for the last five years, at least until he'd met Sunny Patronski at a Cape May restaurant. Things got complicated.

He was happy about the relationship but the timing was bad. They fell in love as the project was reaching its climax, and for more weekends than he liked to admit, the Technical Center had taken precedence over his visits with Sunny at her Cape May, New Jersey, condo on Beach Drive. He did not like the feeling that this was going to be another one of those weekends.

"Are you serious? It wasn't dead on the numbers?" Harmond asked.

"Sure am, sir. No problem if you want to go to Canada. I can land at Erie International, talk to customs, get a clearance. Great croissants at the Mofatt Inn there, just outside Niagara On The Lake."

"You lie," Harmond said. "Pulling my chain. Come on, Butch. This isn't funny. It has to be okay. I'm just about the only guy on this now. Clark Dowler is out of commission with some kind of weird amnesia."

"Seriously, Mr. Harmond, last time this happened the weather was going down and the glideslope component, both horizontal and vertical, was off, so I switched to the old system. I had to put some of those little yellow sticky notes on your radios and indicators just to hide those lying numbers and keep them from distracting me. Otherwise I'd have ended up trying to make like a seaplane in Lake Ontario. And I don't have a seaplane rating."

"That's okay, Butch, this Citation can make water landings—only one, though." His joke didn't help. No one laughed.

"What were you doing up there in Canada, Butch?"

"Bart and I were flying GOD to Toronto," Dominion said.

The copilot looked over at them and nodded his head in the affirmative. He then pointed to the off-course heading on the gyro and wet compass.

"GOD?" Harmond said. "Lack of oxygen, hypoxia can cause some strange things, gentlemen."

"GOD is the Geodesic Office Of Dialectics," Butch explained. "The acronym means nothing. It's part of the title for their newsletter. You ever read one and you'll see it doesn't make much sense. They just like the ring of it.

"These brains on the trip were out of a think tank near Syracuse. Mostly a bunch of retired college professors. I don't mean to be disrespectful, Mr. Harmond, but they were just really kinda' strange. Harmless but strange.

"They were very interested in the WAAS, but it was honest academic interest. One of these guys crawled up to the front office. Tapped me on the shoulder. He was a little airsick. We were up and down in some pretty nasty thermals. Then we were into some severe chop and he didn't want to stand up. Said he liked it better low to the deck, so he crawled."

Dominion reached into his khaki cargo pants and took out a roll of mints, unraveled them and extended his hand to Harmond. "Breath mint, sir," he said.

"Don't stop now, Butch. You have my attention."

"Well, the guy looks at the numbers your WAAS is putting out. Then he looks at the hash marks on his handheld GPS, about a $300 item he brought just for kicks, and he gets real quiet, stands up and bangs his head on the bulkhead.

He says, 'Captain'—I liked him calling me Captain—'you're off course.'"

Matt got down on his knees between the pilots. "My attention is undivided, Captain, " he said.

"Thank you, sir. Well, Mr. Harmond, I tell Bart to take the stick. I take out my whiz wheel, flight computer and an old Magellan GPS from my flight bag and start comparing numbers. Now don't get me wrong, boss. I like working for you. This old guy though was on the money. My ol' GPS crosschecked with his and all the other gauges told me your stuff was lying. You know what they say: Trust your instruments. Well I sure couldn't trust these. But the real problem was that the new system almost had us believing in it. It looked like the numbers were, as you say, dead balls on target.

"Now that's no big deal in visual flight rules. But put me off a degree or two or three and then have my instruments lie to me when I can't see in front of my nose, and we have big-time shit-storm problems. I don't like to think about it.

"So, thank God, no pun intended, I didn't look at your machine. I looked at the handheld GPS info. Otherwise I'm not sure what would have happened other than eating croissants in Canada."

Matt saw Bart in the copilot's seat shrug his shoulders.

"I just work here," the copilot said. "I sit over here in the right seat and do my duty. Mind if I smoke?" he said. "Just kidding."

"Very funny," Matt said. "Take us home, Butch."

"Sir? You mean home as in our destination, Cleveland?"

"No Butch. I mean home as in Atlantic City. The Center O' Enlightenment. I have to see the boss. And Butch, get out a visual flight rules sectional chart to keep us out of trouble. Turn on WAAS. Follow it. See where it takes us for a while."

Dominion reached into his flight case, extracted a ragged map and opened it. "This has to be three years old," he said. "We never need these things in this kind of ass-kicking machine. We don't see many landmarks at 40,000 feet."

"I know. Just humor me," Matt said.

Dominion switched on the WAAS display, and it lit up the panel in front of them with intersecting red and green lines. A moving map display appeared with latitudes, longitudes and all the information they needed to complete their flight to their home airport in Atlantic City, or for that matter, any airport in the contiguous U.S.

Matt leaned over and pointed to the heading the WAAS was telling them to fly as an on-course routing to their home destination. Dominion turned the yoke of the Citation and picked up the course.

They looked outside into a perfect blue sky.

"There's the coast," Mr. Harmond. "There's the skyline over there. WAAS is telling me to turn south to get on course. That'll take us to the Carolinas somewhere. Nice place, the Outer Banks. Guess we could have lunch at the Pelican Club there."

"Shit," Harmond said. "Look at the frigging map."

3

Bertrum Randolph opened a bag of Fig Newtons. He'd finished what he perceived as a health food meal consisting of Hi-C and toasted cheese he'd made with an iron. Dessert was also healthy.

He bit into the first cookie as he scanned five dusty computer monitors. They were antiques, but all online. None had familiar icons on the screens signifying virus or firewall protection. They were naked in a vicious cyber world, open to the whims of any hacker who wanted to hack for fun or profit. They remained on 24-hours a day. He had to see what worked and what didn't work at circulating the electro poisons he spread for fun and more recently for profit.

Randolph had been part of the infamous SoBig.F, a virus sent to hundreds of millions of unsolicited e-mail addresses around the world. It was the high point of his life since he'd spread his first primitive virus on a floppy disk in 1987. It spread, but only when floppy disks were exchanged. But the SoBig.F viral flood disrupted businesses from Time Warner to Starbucks, and that was only the beginning. Encrypted in the coded virus was a second stage set for attack in a week. That's what he loved—the double whammy.

A worldwide network of virus hunters had attempted to crack the encryption of the most sophisticated virus in history. Britain's Sophos P.L.C., Tokyo's Trend Micro, Symantec and Network Associates in California as well as Microsoft and Computer Associates in Long Island and the renowned F-Secure in Helsinki all attempted to stop the viruses.

As he munched the Fig Newton, one of the dinosaurs rebooted—the reboot initiated by one of his viruses.

Watching all the honey pot screens get blitzed like this is some kind of voyeur-cyber-masturbation, he thought. *Just beginning. Encrypted second stage next week. I need milk.*

He took the glass of milk to a group of card tables. They were filled with Global Positioning Systems and one laptop.

Codes, encryptions, aeronautical charts, instrument approaches and en-route routings flickered together in a morass of twisted numbers and letters until the laptop settled onto a clearly printed screen:

Pseudo random noise scrambler, input decode signal modulator, spread spectrum; time and frequency domain.

He double-clicked on fun biohazard 3. The screen displayed a title page: GPS ERRORS—ionospheric delay, orbit model errors, viral dithering; SELECTIVE AVAILABILITY—SELECTIVE DENIABILITY.

He double-clicked on DESIGN ANTENNA and scrolled to PARTS IS PARTS. It read:

HELICAL OR PATCH ANTENNAS
EQUIPMENT LIST
CLIENT DEMO
Microwave anechoic chamber
Network analyzer
Styrofoam sheets
Paper clips
Shampoo bottles
Pie pans
Yogurt cups

"Paper clips," he said. "My little antennas to the world."

The next screen appeared with text across the title page in large red letters:

FOR SALE
SLOW DEGREDATION KILL CYCLE
BEST OFFER

Bertrum smiled. He loved the thought of hurting, technically and physically. Even ending things. Inconvenience and chaos ruled. He licked his fingers, smelled them and took a deep breath. He unzipped his pants and loosened his belt, letting his gut distend. He closed his eyes.

A hypnotic rain fell and he heard it distantly in that mystic place where he slept and didn't sleep. That place where pieces of dreams streamed together with beauty and ugliness, kindness and death.

No chaos for me, he thought. *No uncertainty.* He opened his eyes wide and slapped himself one, two, three times until it hurt and throbbed enough to bring him to a definite consciousness. "I will not be, not be neither here nor there," he mumbled. "And piss on double comparatives, double negatives."

Now he knew what he was, no confusion, no question. He was awake, not asleep. He had to know what he was. Not to know was to be like other assholes. And he would not be an asshole. The others would be rectal vaults of stupidity.

He took his shirt and pants off, then his underwear. He threw them at the cat. "Poor pussy," he said.

He put his feet on the computer table, reached over and grabbed the baby powder—self-assured, in control, knowing. He leaned and sprinkled it under him on the metal chair. He felt the absorbing powder doing its job, going where it would help what was wrong, making it better. He laughed out loud. "I love it," he said. "God bless America!"

He decided not to sleep. Definitely not to sleep. *It is my essence,* he thought. *It is what is real. My nails, my smell, my hair. My essence. What is inside of me makes me perfect for good and perfect for bad.*

He stood and brushed off some powder, lifted his hands to his nose, breathed deeply. Chamomile, vitamin E. Then he slowly lowered to his knees, faced a PC, crossed himself, kissed his middle finger and said, "Give me the power." He raised his hands, extended his middle finger and smiled. "Good night, sweet prince. Good night."

4

Somewhere over Gettysburg the solvent odor entered Sunny's nostrils. *It was incongruous,* she thought, *home repair smells at altitude with Clayton Meadows in a bag.*

She wondered where it had been hiding for the first part of her flight from Cape May to Allegheny County. *Carl must have cleaned up some of it,* she thought. *Otherwise, why solvent, and wouldn't that sort of thing hinder genetic stuff or whatever it is forensic labs do?*

Her mind wondered about color—the color of the body paint, brand name, stirring stick, price? Was it on sale? Why paint or turpentine? What the hell happened?

She thought about turning back and canceling the flight plan, but she pictured the airport at Cape May—deserted, no ambulance to take her passenger off her hands, no Carl with a dirty yellow tie, nowhere to go with the corpse. Not a real viable option to take it home for the night. Where do you return such cargo? She knew she was committed, like driving through a tunnel—one entrance, one exit. Her salvation was the light at the end of the flight. At least it was something to do on a Saturday night. What a date.

Weather from flight service was correct: severe clear from Cape May to Pittsburgh. She scanned the Multifunction Display on the moving map and entertained her mind with the bright green-and-pink course line extending from Cape May to Allegheny County. She scanned lightning strike mode, traffic standby and clear skies module. She opened her flight bag and took out a stick of gum, jamming the wrapper into her purse. She heard the noise of her chewing reverberate in the headphones. She spit the gum into a Kleenex.

Sunny looked to the left of the panel at the glass cockpit primary flight display. Everything she needed was there: nav, bearing, range, heading, attitude. *Everything but my damn date,* she thought.

Earlier, before the neighborly call from Carl, Sunny believed she had the weekend made. She had been looking out over the yard in front of her condo. Beyond the small garden area was a sidewalk, then Beach Drive and finally white, soft sand welcoming the Atlantic. She thought about how things could not get much better.

She had 15 menus, all from Cape May restaurants, on a green plastic table beside her. Her cell phone rested atop the pile and held them down in the stiff summer ocean wind.

Eleven of the menus were gourmet, including some five-star restaurants. She counted them, stacked them according to price, then motif—a little girl planning her picnic. There were also quaint lunch places, the kind with checkered tablecloths, empty wine bottles with candles stuck in them and multicolored dried wax molded to the sides.

The lighting will be dim and soft blues will play in the background. He'll flirt with the waitress and I'll pretend I'm jealous. Matt won't want to go out for breakfast on Sunday. Maybe just have a cappuccino and danish from Quick Mart in Wildwood Crest.

Wind whipped around the corner of her condo at Maycomb Beach. It was already 87 humid summer degrees at seven in the morning.

A middle-aged man and woman stood a few feet from the ocean doing some sort of yoga or tai chi. Sunny looked up at them, then back to the menus, planning. The contrast in temperature between stiff breeze and hot coffee made steam rise then disappear in a horizontal thrust into the atmosphere. She leaned over the hot brew and breathed in the aroma, half French vanilla, half regular decaf.

Dinner would be at The Pendergrass Inn, then a walk on the night beach at Cape May. Tomorrow would be lunch at The Flower Pot and a short flight with Matt to Atlantic City in her Cirrus for some conservative gambling and laughs.

Life will be good.

It was the first ring of her cell phone sitting on top of the menus that had jolted her out of the daydream planning.

"Sunny, it's me, Matt. You up?"

She watched the menus blow off the deck when she picked up the cell.

"More than up," she said. "I'm sort of fantasizing. Third cup of coffee."

"Sounds good to me," he said.

"I mean I was looking at menus, Matt," she said. "Just that kind of food orgasm fantasizing. Hmmmm. But I'm fantasizing about other kinds, too."

There was a silence on the phone.

"That's why I'm calling, Sunny. I hate to say this. It's about our weekend. I have to get there late, maybe postpone. I'm not sure yet."

She stood and walked toward the menus scattered over the grass.

"What's that noise?" he asked.

"It's just me spinning myself into the ground. Just looking for something to do. No, I'm picking up menus on the lawn. Matt, this was supposed to be so special."

"I can't explain it all now," Matt said. "Clark Dowler—something happened. It's called dissociative fugue, a form of amnesia. I'm covering for him. He's not going to be back for a while. At least we don't think. Everything's sketchy.

"This fugue is weird, Sunny. You don't just forget, you lose your identity. Actually, the shrink said you form a new one. Hell, a brain surgeon could end up a farmer, start an entirely new life and remember nothing of the life he just walked away from."

Sunny looked at the bars disappearing on her cell phone. "Signal getting weak here, Matt. I'll get up to the third-floor deck. Wait," she said.

Sunny left the menus blowing in circles on the grass, put her coffee mug down and ran into the condo and up the stairs to her bedroom. She pulled open the sliding glass doors and stood on the wind-blown deck looking at one bar, two bars, then three on the cell.

"I have to go, Sunny. They're waiting for me. I'll call if I can be there this weekend at all. I don't know. I should be able to get back to you later this morning."

"Go?" she said. "Where are you going? What's going on? It's our weekend," she said.

She turned off the cell. It rang again. It wasn't Matt. "Howdy do there, Sunny?" the voice said. "Your friendly neighbor here with a request."

Turbulence shook Sunny back to the reality of the flight. She liked that. No fooling around, no feeling sorry, just the authenticity of wind, temperature, visibility and speed.

She tightened her safety harnesses, double-checked the pink course line, glanced at the engine monitor, flipped off the S-TEC autopilot and looked at a perfect GPS-inspired navigation line. Like Matt would say, dead balls on course.

"Just a minute, Sunny," she said to herself. "Crosscheck your stuff, girl. Redundancy saves lives."

Crosscheck and redundancy did it this time; the sound of the words he'd used so many times when he was teaching her to fly. It was always some sort of key that toggled a brain synapse in Sunny's head, some fleshy microcircuit to materialize memories of the gentle and wrinkled face of her grandfather. It was a picture she saw, a photo hanging above her fireplace at the condo.

There were two poster-sized photos, both in matching Victorian frames. The photo on the left was of her mother and father. Both had died in a boating accident shortly after she was born. The large color poster showed them standing in the ocean on a cool fall morning dressed in rubber diving gear, fishing for sand sharks at Wildwood Crest, just south of the amusement park. In the distance through the ocean mist you could see silhouettes of the Wildwood rides.

The photo to the right was of her grandmother and grandfather sitting on the beach in front of their condo at Maycomb Beach. It was a dull and overcast day and they were dressed in bright swim gear, relaxing on beach chairs. Above the ocean waves an old J-3 banner-towing plane moved over the beach. It trailed a sign that read, *LOBSTER, ALL YOU CAN EAT AT THE CRAB HOUSE. HOME OF THE BIG CRABS.*

She thought of her grandfather and grandmother every day but was never sure when a word or the sight of a particular airplane would trip the circuitry and play the memories. The ride to the airport triggered it this time. The movie played in her head: the hangar parties, working on engines, learning to keep from cutting her hands on wires and metal when she stood beside him wanting to help. At first, she did not even know how to hold a wrench or screwdriver. But she learned, and by the time she was a junior in high school, she not only had her private license, she was right there beside him digging into whatever needed to be done.

Sunny's grandparents were generous, leaving her the plane and condo. There wasn't much money. William Ramsey Powell and his wife, Greta, knew how to live, spend and enjoy. So what was left was both material and spiritual. Assets but no cash. There was the plane and condo and memories of an introspective grandfather and grandmother.

"N834C Delta," a voice boomed in her headset. "You changing your on-course heading, Delta? You have a request?"

The sound of the controller's voice startled Sunny. Flying was no place to be swept into some sort of sentimental somnolence and lose your way. This is where she was supposed to shine, as her grandfather used to say.

"No, ah, sir....Assigned heading of 278 degrees is fine. Compass must be precessing. I'll reset."

The controller came back. "Turn left. Intercept the Revloc nine-two radial for traffic avoidance. Expect direct to AGC."

Sunny looked outside, crosschecked her compass, GPS and everything else she could find to crosscheck. She was in fact on course. She tried to imagine that Pittsburgh Approach was wrong, yet she knew that seldom happened. "Trust your instruments," her grandfather used to say. "They don't lie. Believe them."

But he also explained to her there were instances of pilots accepting clearances, turning to assigned headings from a controller and then politely flying into the side of a mountain, simply because they weren't thinking.

"You're the pilot in command, Sunny girl. You use your head. Crosscheck and do what you believe is right. I believe in you. You have to believe in yourself."

She talked to herself. It made things make more sense when flying alone. Well, technically alone. She looked over at Meadows packaged in the body bag. Correction, crime scene recovery bag.

She looked outside at the clear skies. The glow of Christmas-like lights lit up Greensburg, Jeanette and Rostraver. Further to the northwest she saw the lights of Allegheny County and beyond that the crisscrossing runways of Pittsburgh International.

Let's see, she thought, *all the towns are where they're supposed to be, the roads—good shape. Miss you Grampaw. Really do. Where the hell are you, Matt?*

5

Captain Lorraine Harding kissed her husband goodbye on a perfect Saturday evening. She picked up her son and tilted him horizontally, turned and banked him—an airliner on perfect approach.

She ran her hand across his mouth, cleaned away some peanut butter, and kissed him. "Mummy will see you in a couple days, honey. You be good for Daddy."

"Bring me something back, Mum. A present," he said.

"We'll see. Maybe."

The boy turned and ran back to the house. Lorraine's husband, Gerald Harding, an unemployed mechanical-engineer-turned-house-dad, grabbed his wife and pulled her close. He pretended to wipe something from her lips and kissed her.

"Honey, the neighbors," she said, pushing him away.

"I'll kiss them later. Love the one you're with."

She gently slapped him on the face and laughed. She picked up her suitcase and headed for the Volvo station wagon. There were soccer stickers plastered on the windows and rear bumper. A vanity plate on front of the car read "MOM's SOCCER TAXI."

She put her window down as she pulled out of the driveway and extended her hand to wave.

"You going to wave again?" her husband asked. Gerald Harding threw both his hands into the air, trying to flag her down. He screamed for her to stop. There was a screech of brakes as a Corvette swerved to miss the Volvo. Captain Harding came to an abrupt stop, her head snapping against the headrest.

"Well, Captain, better get clearance before exiting the driveway," Gerald said. He walked over to the car, reached in, held her head gently and kissed her once more.

Lorraine Harding had been promoted to captain three months earlier. Her bump to the new position was not unexpected. She'd worked for years to build the hours in order to be considered for the left seat. There was bush pilot time in Alaska, flying checks out of Cleveland in all sorts of bad weather and in all sorts of bad equipment. She instructed student pilots on weekends, and for a time performed in local air shows and fly-ins doing aerobatics in her Pitts Special. She was an excellent pilot, calm under pressure and self-assured. Fellow pilots and ground personnel at Air Cargo Express liked her and were happy to see her well-deserved promotion. Today, however, she would be flying with First Officer Duane Carlson Blaster.

Blaster wasn't passed over for promotion because of his female competition. There was no comparison in terms of pilot-in-command hours. Lorraine Harding had twice as many hours as her chauvinistic competition. She hadn't stepped on any toes, but Blaster didn't care. All women had a place, and it wasn't at the controls of a Boeing 767-300 Freighter with two Pratt & Whitney engines and 63,300 pounds of thrust each.

Captain Harding knew she had to be ready for her first officer. She had to psych herself up every time she flew with him, and she did not want to have to be bothered with interpersonal relations when she had more than enough to keep her mind occupied.

She had opted to go with air cargo carriers rather than passenger airlines because she didn't want to deal with drunken, obnoxious, incipient passengers onboard her flights. The captain was ultimately responsible and she was aware how much of a captain's job involved dealing with the unruly, pissed off, I-have-my-rights public.

What had become an emotional ordeal between her and First Officer Blaster was just the type of thing she wanted to avoid. Their flights usually became a male-female macho competition for her copilot, and she didn't like it. There was enough to think about with more than 4,000 cubic feet of cargo cutting through the atmosphere at 530 miles an hour. Besides, Pittsburgh weather was ceiling and visibility unlimited. Her destination weather was going down the tubes.

When Lorraine Harding ran into her first officer, he was sipping coffee at a Wendy's in the Pittsburgh International Airport's Airmall. She decided to try to get along with this man—no matter what it took.

"Duane, hi. Good to see you," she lied.

"Can I get you a coffee, Captain—ma'am?" he said.

She bit her lower lip hard and wondered if it would bleed.

"Sure, thanks," she said.

Duane Blaster stood up and extended his hand.

"Fresh start," he said. "No hard feelings, aye?"

They shook hands and Harding felt Blaster's middle finger gouge into the palm of her right hand as they shook. It went back and forth and he didn't let go. He raised his eyebrows and smiled as he kept stroking her palm with the thick muscular finger. She felt his nail dig in. She looked him in the eye and frowned.

"Duane, stop it. What are you doing? That's enough."

She pulled her hand back. He wouldn't let go. He clenched tighter and laughed. She put her left hand on his wrist and tried to shake it loose. She pulled hard at the same time he released his tight grip, lost her balance and fell backward, stepping as fast as she could to keep from falling. She had pulled too hard to escape his strong grip and couldn't stop the fall.

A little girl with blonde ponytails pointed. "Look, Mommy. Look at the lady on the ground."

"Mind your own business, Sally. She just fell. That's all."

Lorraine looked at the girl and smiled as she picked herself off the floor. Blaster walked over to her, stood directly above, uncomfortably close, spread his legs and extended a hand.

"Here, Captain, let me help. Did you fall and can't get up?"

Lorraine pushed herself away from the crotch looming above her. She stood up and with both hands dusted herself off.

Blaster moved closer. "Here, let me help," he said.

"No, get away, please. I'm just fine."

"Gee, Captain, I hope this isn't a sign of things to come. Here, let me go get you that coffee. Looks like you need it. Need something."

"No thanks, Duane. I'm fine. We better get to the 300. Weather is going down at destination. We get in a little early we might be able to avoid the worst of it. No big deal. Just might make things more pleasant."

"Yes, ma'am. Whatever you say ma'am, sir."

With a bastard file, pair of tin-snips and needle-nose pliers, Bertrum Randolph continued his construction of a demo GPS for one of his prospective clients. The object wasn't to show them how to use the admittedly primitive unit; rather it was to let them know how advanced his methods had become since the meteoric rise in global positioning technology.

He stood happily naked and powdered in front of the computers. The cutters slipped and pushed a paper clip into his finger. A small amount of blood dotted the prick.

"Ouch! Son of a bitch! Fuck. Just for that"—he pointed the primitive homemade antenna to the sky—"maybe I'll dump one in the drink today. Part of the demo. Just for chuckles. No charge."

6

"*Wacker* is the damn magazine the article was in," Matt said to his boss, Dr. Wilhamena Halstead. "There was an entire article on hacking into GPS signals, like it was some kind of computer game, like there were no lives at stake. I experienced it today, Dr. Halstead. It is not just a magazine article to me anymore."

"Sit down, Matt," she said. "You have to be tired. You're doing too much, really you are. You just landed."

Dr. Wilhamena Halstead looked to see that the door to her office was closed. She walked around her desk and moved close to Matt. She patted his blushing face with her long fingers. He knew she was going to move in closer. She always did.

Her tight skirts, thin sweaters and high heels had become legendary around the office. To Matt's friends she was The Shark and the shoes were fuck-me shoes. To Matt they were a nuisance, just as they were to any of the younger males under her supervision.

Sunny and The Shark first met at a Christmas party. It was the second time Matt and Sunny had been out and although they were not yet intimate, it was obvious to Sunny that her date's boss was on his trail; actually, she was on every male's trail.

They joked about it on the way home to Sunny's condo on Beach Drive, but ever since the Christmas party, Sunny knew all about the aspirations of Dr. Wilhamena Halstead.

Dr. Halstead angled herself between Matt and her desk and stood directly in front of him, motionless, waiting. Nothing happened in the awkward silence. She slapped her hands together, startling Matt.

"Well then, Matt, we'll be having a meeting. We can air our discord there.

Everyone will be given their fair time. We'll decide where to go once we hear from everyone."

"Dr. Halstead, the article is technically competent. Celeste is making copies now. For Christ's sake, they can build a low-cost jammer out of components they get at any mall tech store and grocery store."

"Don't overreact, Matt. I'm sure everything will come out in the end. We're no Mickey Mouse outfit here, you know."

She was right about that. With an agency budget reaching into the stratosphere and a building that put the White House to shame, it was one of the most abundantly funded operations in the DOT.

Located ten miles northwest of Atlantic City, The William J. Hughes Technical Center covered more than 5,059 acres with state-of-the-art laboratories and test facilities. In addition, the Center was the location of the Federal Air Marshal Program and The Transportation Security Laboratory, which is the government's leading test and evaluation facility for improving airport security technology. Since the events of September 11, it has also become the key location for Homeland Security.

Programs include evaluation of air traffic control, navigation, aircraft safety, security and communications. There is long-range development of innovative systems and concepts, development of new air traffic control equipment and software and modification of existing systems and procedures. At any one time there are at least 150 projects underway at the facility. For all intents and purposes, it is the Federal Aviation Administration's Pentagon. Economically, there are 1,650 federal employees along with 1,300 contract employees. The combined annual payroll is in excess of $129.6 million plus an additional $319 million in other related activities.

Dr. Halstead brushed up against Matt's shoulder and circled around to his rear. "You'll have your chance, Matt. Don't worry," she said, and patted him on the shoulder.

7

Underneath the 170-foot wingspan of the Boeing 767 Freighter, Captain Lorraine Harding attempted to complete her customary preflight of the 450,000-pound jet. She rubbed her sore hip and attempted to hide the limp as a result of her fall at Wendy's.

"Concentration—focus," she said to herself, trying to forget the incident in the terminal building. She was aware the two-crew Boeing could be a lonely place if two personalities were not on the same page, especially if they were flying a North Atlantic Los Angeles-London or Newark-Moscow leg.

Thus far, she had been able to fly most of her flights on domestic routes in order to keep family life disruptions to a minimum. But as cargo layoffs loomed in the future, she was uncertain as to how long she could afford to be picky.

She walked into the wide-bodied jet, limping between 60 tons of cargo pallets. A few lights remained on within the expansive bulkhead of the ship, but since the placement of the last pallet and battening down of the large cargo door on the main deck of the forward fuselage, there were just shadows and the eternal whine of generators. She didn't like the absence of windows in the fuselage. But if she were going to fly freighters to avoid dealing with passengers, some concessions would have to be made.

Her first officer shouted "Howdy!" when he saw her shadow behind him. He was in the right seat with his head down, looking into a checklist.

"Hello," she said.

"The weather has gone down at destination, Captain."

"Please, Duane," she said. "Call me Lori."

"The weather has gone down at destination, Captain Lori."

Lorraine Harding rolled her eyes toward the top of the cabin. She took a deep breath and silently let it out so First Officer Blaster could not detect her frustration. "Thanks, Duane. We'll be fine. We're on the new system. No problem," she said. "The WAAS and the LAAS. Doesn't get much better than this." She paused. "Duane, I've been meaning to talk to you," Harding said.

"Talk away, Captain Lori Harding. Talk away." Blaster's eyes stayed focused on the checklist.

"I feel uncomfortable. I mean I feel uncomfort—"

"Then squirm around in your seat. Take a few breaths. Fill those lungs up. Expand if you can. That'll make you more comfy," Blaster said.

"That's not what I mean, Duane. You know what I'm saying. You're not looking at me. Not paying attention."

"Oh my," Blaster said as he tucked the checklist between his legs, folded his hands and placed them on his lap. "There. Better now? I'm all ears. What must you have to say that's so very important?"

Harding twisted in her seat to face him. "This isn't working, Duane. The relationship is not only counterproductive, it is potentially dangerous."

"Just be more careful when you're at a Wendy's, Captain. You lost your balance. I know it could have been a dangerous situation, but you made it. And watch out for that steaming hot coffee. You heard about that old lady who got scalded after taking a sip of her coffee at one of those fast food places? She sued and I think she won. But the burns. My God. Her poor old lap, all funny now. Probably hard for her to get a date. By the way. Your stay-at-home-and-do-the-dishes hubby still there?"

Lorraine looked into Blaster's eyes. He did not look away. Both waited for the other to speak. Harding's head moved up and down slightly. Deadpan eyes. She was trying not to react; trying to wait, feeling a swelling in her throat.

She had cried once during the early days of her flight training. And that was enough. There were the sexist comments, snickers, laughs and off-color jokes told so she could hear them. They grew dirtier as the months of flight training went on. A couple of the men she trained with told the jokes directly to her. The worst was when one of them would sit and sip coffee with her at a corner table in the pilots' lounge and tell the filthiest ones, then reach over and touch her. It felt dirty and dark.

That was enough for her. She had vowed never to let it happen again. To deal with the periodic unpleasantness, she had started reading self-help books and learned defense mechanisms. No matter how simple they were, no matter how ridiculous, she took the recommendations. They worked.

She made herself emotionally transparent, letting the anger and pain flow through her. She accepted the moment and what it brought and instead of trying to make it go away, she simply made herself aware.

"This isn't the time or place," she said. "I made a mistake. Shouldn't have brought it up here. Not now. Not healthy, I...."

First Officer Blaster slid out of his right seat position. "I have to take a leak, Captain. Here, hold this."

He leaned over Harding and quickly shoved the checklist between her legs. He spoke slowly. "Just be a minute. Keep that warm."

He turned to leave, then stopped in front of her, his crotch close to her face. He lingered for an eternal second.

Harding pulled the plastic checklist from between her legs and threw it. She missed. Blaster turned around when he saw the plastic fly past him. He bent over and picked it up. "Temper now there, Lorraine. Temper. We have a long night ahead of us."

She gazed out the front of the Freightliner at the mechanics, linemen and fuel trucks. She folded her hands on her lap, closed her eyes and pictured her home, her son and Gerald.

"Okee-dokee, Captain. Rock and roll," Blaster said as he slid into the right seat of the 767. "May I have my checklist, please? Oh my. Nice and warm."

8

The cellular sitting on Sunny's lap vibrated at the same time she keyed the push-to-talk button. The lights of Pittsburgh appeared in front of her as she anticipated her clearance into Allegheny County. She took her hand off the push-to-talk switch and answered the cellular. She'd had no anxiety pings and hadn't heard a word from her passenger in the bag. Perspiration was down to nil and it looked to her as though Pittsburgh was going to be a non-event.

She held the phone tightly against her ear. "Sunny," Matt said. "Have I got news for you."

"I don't know. Do you?" She said it with that sarcastic, we're-about-to-break-up voice. She didn't like her own tone. She decided to try and make it go away, to change the feelings, including the inflection of her voice.

"I have to tell someone. No, I have to tell you, Sunny. I don't care if the phone is secure or not," he said. "First, I quit. Second, I have to tell you about the WAAS and LAAS stuff. This country could be in bigger trouble than we could ever imagine. Where are you?"

Sunny looked at the distance measuring equipment in the Cirrus and realized she was getting uncomfortably close to PIT and AGC and needed to be talking to someone in the controlled airspace. She was aware there were fighters out there ready to scramble if she stepped into the wrong airspace.

There were more than 30,000 aircraft in and out of Pittsburgh per year, and that traffic didn't include the activity at surrounding airports. She heard her grandfather's patient, kind, gravely words in her mind—*Aviate, fly the airplane first, then navigate, then communicate. Remember, f.t.f.a., fly the friggin' airplane, honey. Then you can navigate. Then communicate on the radio.*

Sunny looked down at route 279 which, if she followed it, would go directly past PIT. But she wasn't on a visual flight rules flight plan. She was in the system and had to remain in compliance with instrument flight rules. There was no following a stream of traffic below her and easily letting it lead her to her destination airport.

She waited for her assigned heading from Pittsburgh's Approach Control. Although she was landing at Allegheny with her corpse, she needed a clearance from PIT. She would then be handed off to Allegheny Tower for her approach and landing. Approach first, corpse later.

Sunny still hadn't answered Matt's question. There was silence on the line. She was distracted with no clearance, approaching controlled airspace, heavy-metal traffic looming in front of her and a cadaver in one of Carl Farnley's wonderful crime scene disaster recovery bags beside her.

"Just about over Pittsburgh," she finally said into the cell. Again, with a tone of voice she didn't want to hear herself use, she added, "Why do you ask?"

"Why?" Matt said. "I mean, why are you there? And why are you talking on a cell phone when you're in the air? Isn't there a law or something?"

"It's a cell phone, not a bomb, for God's sake. And I'm no airliner. My date is right here beside me. Clayton can't talk right now, though. He's, I guess you could say, indisposed, probably for, oh, let's see—eternity."

"What?" Matt said. "What do you mean I have to go with you? I quit." Sunny heard Matt's words, but he wasn't talking to her. The volume was low on her phone. She clicked volume a few times to boost the sound.

"Matt, what'd you say?" she said. "Say again."

She heard a slamming noise like a car door. There was the sound of feet scuffling on pavement.

"Wait a minute, you can't take my phone. I quit! I'm a citizen, for God's sake! What is this? You some kind of Gestapo?"

"This way, Mr. Harmond," Sunny heard a barely distinguishable voice say. "Dr. Halstead requires you at a meeting."

"Fuck her," Matt said, "and the lame horse she rode in on."

Sunny heard the voices chuckling. She didn't hear Matt's familiar laugh.

9

Pat Shepherd, director of security for the Hughes facility, stood in front of a prodigious mahogany table replete with brass nameplates, bottled water, ice buckets and one ashtray. The crystal ashtray was in front of Dr. Halstead's seat at the head of the rectangular portion of the keyhole. It was the only ashtray.

The circular—think Knights of the Round Table—portion attached seamlessly to Dr. Halstead's head position. She sat alone, facing the administrators from each department: Testing and Evaluation; Air Traffic Communications; Navigation; Airport Safety; Security; Systems and Concepts; Homeland Security; Federal Air Marshals; Transportation Security Laboratory; and finally, Group Air Station-U.S. Coast Guard, Atlantic City.

Department heads, assistants and confidential secretaries entered sporadically, each mumbling about late notification and pressing issues. They spoke in respectfully low tones for Dr. Halstead to only hear secondarily what the complaints were.

Matt walked in, one security guard in front of him, another with his hand on Matt's arm. *His date for the meeting*, Matt thought.

He looked at the six-foot-six-inch guard. "You're not quite petite enough for me, grumpy," Matt said.

He tugged his arm and broke the grip. Dr. Halstead looked at the three men entering through the expanse of a ten-foot oak doorway. She saw a look of angry determination form on Matt's face. She gestured at the security types with her hands like she was shooing a fly. Power woman taking care of the small stuff.

"That's just fine, gentlemen. That will be all. You can wait outside."

Matt brushed his coat, whisking away not dust or lint, but rather the negative emotional turmoil created from being accosted like some common criminal.

He walked directly to Pat Shepherd, the ex-Special Forces Force Recon-type in charge of security and heading up the logistical component of the Federal Air Marshals.

"What kind of shit is this, Pat?" Matt said. "I'm under arrest or what?"

Pat took two steps back and raised his hands as though surrendering to the accusation. "Wait a minute there, partner. What are you talking about?"

He walked over and stopped close to Matt. He leaned and whispered in his ear, making sure Halstead wasn't looking. "Her Repugnance requested your presence," he said.

Matt laughed and felt his heart lighten at his friend's joke about Halstead. Her Repugnance. Nice. Just another name for The Shark.

Pat was the only security person Matt could tolerate. Actually he was one of the only people at the Hughes Center Matt enjoyed being around.

Pat had won Matt's loyalty on one long flight in the Cessna Citation. Both were needed in Denver, Matt for WAAS interface problems and Pat for security issues involving what was thought to be simple vandalism at some local airports. The flight home had been diverted because of weather, and while the men tried to kill some time in St. Louis, Matt bought a bottle of Merlot. He uncorked it and they both looked at each other and simultaneously said, "What the hell."

They drank it on the connecting flight and Pat began to share some war stories. They were just good-ol'-boy tales at first, but Pat's reminiscing grew blacker as the Merlot bottle emptied. Pat knew he was responsible for the deaths of at least 10,000 people in Vietnam, both enemy and civilians. His job had been to infiltrate enemy territory and radio coordinates to the jet jocks delivering ordnance, including napalm. He'd seen the results of his work when he was in country on stealth ground missions. It didn't bother him when he was in the midst of surviving the war. But after he returned home, the post trauma started taking its toll.

The mixture of Merlot, the dark jet night and Pat's need to talk linked the men in a short time. Pat had never told anyone before how much his past bothered him. Matt was the only one.

Now, having been delivered by force to the conference room, Matt fumed and wanted answers from his friend.

"This is news to me, Matt. I just got here. I was golfing in Rio Grande. Look at me!"

Pat did his best imitation of a male model, turning around ungracefully and gesturing at his yellow golf pants, hideous socks and corporate logoed golf shirt. "Do I look like security?" he said.

"Oh," Matt said. Pat made a motion with his right hand, pointed to it with his left index finger and said, "Shark fin." He gestured at Dr. Halstead. "It was The Shark who made it happen."

Both men laughed and pulled up chairs as far away from Halstead as they could.

"Mr. Harmond," Dr. Halstead said, slapping her hands together, a displeased teacher ready and willing to whack her unruly students. The smack jarred Matt out of the good mood he'd almost regained in talking with Pat. "Are you ready to start the meeting? I understand you had something to bring to the attention of the staff."

Matt looked at Pat. He stood slowly. "Ah, Dr. Halstead, I hadn't prepared anything formally. We were just talking earlier. I didn't, uh, know you were, uh, going to call this meeting for today."

"You're a big boy, Mr. Harmond. Share with us what you've discovered. I'm sure we will all listen with baited breath. We *all* want to hear. It is our pleasure to give you the floor."

Matt felt his friend kick him under the table. Then he heard Pat whisper, "I'd say you're shark bait, buddy. Suck it up. Deal with it. We'll drink later. Kill the pain."

"Mr. Shepherd, did you have something for the group that you would like to share?" Dr. Halstead said. "Please, share with all. We have plenty of time."

Matt desperately wanted to lean over to Shepherd and say, "That's what you think, Your Grotesqueness."

10

Generally speaking, flying was easy for Captain Harding, especially with the high-tech equipment she loved to have at her fingertips. Even with the onslaught of gray, malignant vapors cutting visibility to zero, there was always the gyroscopic and electrical precision of instrumentation to make it almost a computer game, a colorful and warm experience wrapped within the cockpit.

When the darkness and fog and shafts of lightning attract all attention of those in the front seat of a great 21st-century aircraft, the flip of a switch could make it appear slightly more like a game—cerebral rather than athletic or heroic. There were no silk scarves wafting in the airstream, no leather skullcaps, goggles or high-top leather boots.

It became a matching of lines, grids, ciphers, latitudes and longitudes. It felt good to her because Harding did it well. She was a natural pilot, just as some were natural golfers, swimmers and assassins. Even though the panel sparkled like a game, the perspiration and intense concentration were reminders that it was not.

On this night as Captain Lorraine Harding approached Pittsburgh International Airport from the west, the weather had moved in just as flight service had told her it would earlier in the day. Her first officer was at the controls, hand-flying the aircraft while she dialed in approach frequencies and started the pre-landing checklist.

"PIT Approach, Four-Three-Niner Heavy with you at 15,000," she said into her boom mike.

"Four-Three-Niner, good day, ma'am," the controller said. "Turn to heading 130 degrees. Descend and maintain 10,000."

Captain Harding keyed the mike and acknowledged the descent. "I'll take it, Duane. You handle the radios. I'll hand fly it in," she said.

"It's really getting choppy, Captain. I don't know. You might break a fingernail. Hey, just kidding. You know me."

Lorraine wondered if she had bit her lip too hard again. *Maybe it's really bleeding this time,* she thought. *I have to quit doing this every time this jerk makes a stupid comment.*

She forced a laugh into the intercom. She jiggled her butt down into the seat, a habit she had developed over the years when a difficult landing faced her.

"I love when you do that, Captain," her first officer said. "You know, those Eastern types, the men at least, they drive those car bombs into hotels knowing they will die. You know why?"

"Duane, I'm busy," she said, cutting him off. She wondered if he was intentionally trying to distract her. She was used to being distracted. Most of her instructors tried to do it at the most inopportune times. She knew her concentration was impeccable, but there was more than concentration involved this time. She felt emotions she didn't want to feel. She felt anger at what he was obviously trying to do. Then she stopped. Maybe he wasn't trying to do anything; maybe that's just what this jerk was like.

She didn't like the idea that she was talking to herself when all of her concentration needed to be on the job at hand. Talking out loud was good when flying. She had done that ever since she went to flight school after college. Her first instructor had been a pilot in Vietnam and he encouraged her to talk to herself when going through checklists or making decisions.

Blaster got Harding's attention by keying the mike and making it click in her ear. "Well, I'll tell you exactly why, Captain," he continued. "They really believe they will have ten virgins waiting for them after they die. Hell, I think I'd say that I wanted nine, oh, I don't know, maybe eight virgins. But you can bet your ass I'd want one or two experienced chicks in there, too."

Captain Harding fought to keep control of the large aircraft. She was vectored around some buildups and given a number of heading changes to avoid traffic. The variables of flight accumulated in her mind, but it only amounted to a challenge, something she welcomed. Her first officer, on the other hand, was a pilot of another style. He was amounting to an emotional thermal disturbance and she didn't like it. Distractions could kill. Besides, things just did not seem right to her as she turned to her on-course heading to intercept the instrument landing system.

"PIT," she said into the mike. "Four-Three-Niner with a request."

"Three-Niner Heavy, PIT. Go ahead, Captain."

The controller's voice was calm, unconcerned. He was obviously certain all was going well for Captain Harding and her first officer in the 767.

"Something's funny, Duane. I don't like this. Look at this heading. There's PIT over there. It has to be over there. This can't be right. And look at the speed. Not off much, but off nonetheless, and it won't let me correct."

"You're fine. Look at the LAAS. It's right on the numbers. You'll break out of this stuff in a minute or two. You'll see. You know why else they blow places up, Captain?"

Lorraine Harding ignored him. She looked out of the warm cockpit into the gray night. The Boeing Freighter cut through the fog and moisture, the first officer and controller certain all was accurate on the critical approach into Pittsburgh.

In the distance through the heavy weather, the PPG building's reflective glass façade shined in the driving rain.

11

Three laptops and two desktop PCs glowed in Bertrum Randolph's otherwise darkened apartment in the Strip District of Pittsburgh. His apartment above Klankle's Sandwich and Deli smelled of sauerkraut and fish.

Strapped to his belt was a handheld radio set to scan all frequencies of Pittsburgh Approach Control, including departure and PIT Tower. When activity erupted on any of the frequencies programmed into his radio, the electronic voice activated a stop order in the circuitry. For all intents and purposes, he heard all of the commercial conversations, both those he was permitted to hear and those he was not.

He was on top of every communication between pilot, tower, approach and ground control. If he linked up to one frequency and wanted to keep on it rather than scanning to the next active frequency, he simply pushed a button and the frequency scanning stopped on the active one, the extended conversation between pilot and controller completely available to him.

He came out of the bathroom spooning peanut butter from a jar. After he adjusted the sensitivity of the squelch level on his handheld, he sat down at the PC. He was waiting for a satellite real-time reading that would coincide with his dithering code.

Satellites and their onboard crystal oscillator clocks were used to determine the length of time it took each signal to travel from the satellite to the receiver. That revealed the distance from the station to the satellite.

This information was not rocket science to Randolph. It was basic first-generation satellite GPS knowledge from the launch of TIMATION-I, and in 1969, TIMATION-II.

He liked being up on satellite and GPS information. It made him feel part of the program, part of the crew in that he was current on the latest technology and accessed the same hardware and software those tech types accessed at NASA, the Hughes Center and The Pentagon.

He'd first followed satellite launchings and GPS development with magazine articles and later through Internet research. What especially pleased him was when he used atomic clocks rather than the primitive crystal oscillator clocks from the TIMATION projects. He used his atomic clocks—bought 'em on sale for $39.30—and his used laptops and GPS equipment. He was in the same orbital ballgame as the multimillion-dollar technology crews.

He was aware that the government's atomic clocks onboard the 24 NAVSTAR GPS satellites were rated at an accuracy of one second in 317,000 years. He envied the accuracy, but he'd already determined that close was good enough for his purposes.

He hadn't tested his theory on anything but radio-controlled model aircraft. It was inaccurate, but it worked. His problem in dealing with real aircraft was solved by his inclusion of collocated antennas between his Strip District apartment and Pittsburgh International Airport. It was a somewhat antiquated method, the leapfrog arrangement that scanned the few miles between the two locations. But simple was best.

Unlike earlier Russian hackers who attempted to enter the U.S. GPS satellite timing system, he chose to intercept it as it entered the aircraft, missile, bomb, ship or sub. His only drawback of distance to target had been overcome by what he liked to refer to as the collocated antenna caper.

The antennae appeared harmless enough, and in a world of antennae and radios, especially around an airport the size of PIT, a small and innocuous metal antenna on a billboard or telephone pole appeared totally benign.

He stopped the scan when he heard: "Four-Three-Niner Heavy, turn to 250 degrees, descend and maintain 4,000, intercept and you are cleared for runway 28 Right."

He looked out his window at rain streaming down through a gray and black sky. He opened it and breathed in the smells of the city: baking bread, pizza and bacon below in the deli.

Strewn on the floor beside his chair, covering portions of keyboards and printers, were clippings from newspapers and printouts from Internet media sites, all related to hacking. The most recent headline explained how cyber thieves broke into NASA's computer security defense in addition to the U.S. military's telecommunications network. It read:

"MASTERS OF DAMN DOWNLOADING," OR MODD,

HAVE STRIPPED THE U.S. SPACE AGENCY OF ITS CHIEF DEFENSE AGAINST COMPUTER INTRUSION. THEY HAVE ALSO CLAIMED CREDIT FOR HACKING INTO THE PENTAGON'S DEFENSE INFORMATION SYSTEMS NETWORK (DISN). ACCORDING TO RELIABLE SOURCES, THESE INTRUSIONS WILL PROVIDE THE INTRUDERS WITH ENOUGH INFORMATION TO INFLUENCE MILITARY SATELLITES AND OTHER STRATEGIC SYSTEMS.

The articles were smeared with orange and yellow magic marker, highlighting areas referring to GPS, ATC, APTS (Advanced Public Transit System), ACS (Advanced Control Systems) and DARPA (Defense Advanced Research Projects Agency). One article for the bimonthly hacker magazine *Cyberhunt* contained an article relating to the *Columbia* disaster, explaining the O-ring theory as a complete spoof and typical governmental cover-up.

On the central computer screen was an aerial photo of the William J. Hughes Technical Center in Atlantic City. On the bottom right was the inscription, *Aerial Photo by Bertrum Randolph.*

A female voice interrupted his thoughts as it blared over the radio. It was calm and in control, a sexy beer commercial voice, he thought. "PIT, say again, please?"

"Oh yeah, baby," he mumbled to himself as he reached for the volume control. "Cleared for final?" He quickly swivelled his chair, rolling his way to the row of laptops and PCs. "What the hell. Here goes nothing. Dither me this, bitch."

12

Enveloped in her cocoon somewhere near Pittsburgh, Captain Harding let her head go into that part of her flying experience known as seat-of-the-pants flying instinct. Her instruments told her she was on the LAAS glideslope and glidepath just as she was supposed to be. "Trust your instruments," her flight instructors had always told her. "They don't lie."

On this flight, in the heavy weather going into an international airport in just about zero visibility for the first time, she found her mind beginning to mistrust her heading, altitude and speed.

"Duane, the yoke feels heavy, like my speed isn't up. Feels mushy, like an imminent stall," she said.

"You just need to lift more weights," he said. "You want me to fly it?"

"I got it," she said to him in an angry voice. "And the heading, really, it's way off. This can't be right."

She pointed and touched the directional gyro reading on the glass screen as well as the LAAS distance measuring equipment. "Look at the heading, then the controller turns us in to intercept the glidepath, then he gives us this. Can't be right. We're not headed for the airport."

"Captain Harding," First Officer Blaster said, suddenly serious in his tone, for once not bothering to make a chauvinistic comment. "First rule of flying on the gauges is to trust your instruments," he said. "You know that. For God's sake, lady, fly the fucking approach and believe the expensive instruments you have in front of you. What is your problem?"

"I want to call a missed approach, climb out of here," Captain Harding said.

"I don't feel good about this."

"Lorraine," Blaster snapped back. It was the first time he'd called her by her first name without some sarcastic or melodramatic flare. "Fly the approach and believe what you see in front of you."

Captain Harding keyed the push to talk button. "PIT, Four-Three-Niner Heavy, missed approach," she said into the microphone.

"What's the matter with you? You crazy, lady?" Blaster said. "We don't have to do a go-around. We're supposed to be professionals here. You trying to make us look bad? There's nothing wrong with the approach. Shit, we're exactly where we're supposed to be."

"Duane," Harding shouted into the intercom. "I know where I am and we're not on final going into PIT. I flew for three years out of Beaver County and know this area like the back of my hand. We're not where the instruments are telling us we are."

They looked outside into the gray moisture streaking the windscreen in front of them.

"Three-Niner Heavy, PIT. There a problem? Looking good here," the controller said.

Captain Harding's first officer keyed his mike. "No problem, PIT. We're coming up on the outer marker. We're okay," he said. "Just a slight brain freeze."

The controller keyed his mike and gave a little chuckle for the captain and her first officer to hear.

"I'll take it, Captain," Duane Blaster said. "I want out of this chickenshit assignment with you. Remind me to request an out. Yeah, like I'll really forget."

"Duane, see the glow there? The brightness? I think that's Pittsburgh. I mean the city, not the terminal."

"Bullshit," he said. "Fly the goddamn approach, lady."

13

The last administrator entered the meeting room and sat down beside Matt and Pat Shepherd. It was the only chair left, though Matt would gladly have vacated his hot one at that moment.

"I haven't had any time to prepare anything, Dr. Halstead," Matt said.

"You'll be fine," she said. "Just go with it, young man. We'll listen, and you can be damn sure if you don't have it right, we'll let you know. Now stand up straight."

Pat Shepherd cupped his hands and mumbled to Matt, "Yeah, Matt. Stand erect—shark attack, shark attack."

"Mr. Shepherd," Dr. Halstead said. "That's twice. Do you have a comment? Care to speak on behalf of your friend? Or is there a security issue here you'd like to address?"

"No ma'am. I'm good. A-OK," he said.

Matt took a quick breath and started his presentation to the administrators at the William J. Hughes Technical Center. He kicked it off with a bang.

"Hackers have figured a way to access our LAAS and WAAS systems. They're not safe any longer for use, for sale, for navigation, for approaches or for anything but making lamps out of them, maybe selling them at garage sales."

Matt sat down because he knew it would take awhile before Dr. Halstead got the group under control.

Shepherd leaned over to Matt. "Think you could be any more blunt? Good grief, man, lighten up. Her Protuberance will be pissed."

Matt became aware of his negative body language, like a teenager rebelling against authority, and he didn't like the picture it was painting of his attitude.

A more appropriate portrait would express unadulterated fear.

The room noise was deafening. The security team members who had been standing outside ran into the room with weapons drawn, a wide-eyed look of "kill the intruders" on their faces. They were dressed like a rookie SWAT team and loving it. The tall one was bent at the knees, scanning with his Glock, pre-target recognition like some kind of cop show on prime time.

Pat Shepherd saw his men in the doorway. He stood up. Fortunately his scream could be heard over the noise in the great room. "Jesus H. Christ! Put those guns away! You boys could hurt someone. What is the matter with you? We are the good guys. You work for us. This is our house."

Security bowed their collective heads and holstered their weapons. They turned and walked through the doorway to their place in the hall, puppy dogs having made a mess in the boardroom.

"Sorry, Dr. Halstead. They're young, just want to help. Noise musta' startled 'em," Shepherd said.

"I hope you don't give them real bullets, Pat," she said.

When the room settled down, Matt stood. He leaned in to whisper to Pat. "Can you get my cell phone off those guys, Pat?"

"Calling your dating service, Matt? You probably need one."

"I'm sorry," Matt said. "I didn't mean to be a grandstander, folks. I don't normally run meetings. But I will tell you this. I don't know how to pull any punches here and that is the bottom line no matter how I slice it. Our system can be hacked, even though right now as far as I understand, it is not fine-tuned. The results hackers are getting are somewhat primitive, but nonetheless disturbing. They're currently rough as far as heading changes and altitude readouts. My fear is that it will become more tailored to the uses of those who may want to purchase the technology."

"Where do they get the hardware and software?" a voice asked. "They have it now?"

"Malls, radio supply stores, computer stores," Matt said. "All the necessary technology is coming onto the Internet and there have been some magazine articles. They were bogus before, but if you look at the latest ones, they're on the money."

"Have you tried to build a prototype, Matt?" Dr. Halstead calmly asked as she took a drag off her just-lit, tattooed cigarette.

"Didn't have to. They, or should I say someone, dithered us when we were in the Citation. And I can guarantee it wasn't the President.

"Butch Dominion said it happened to him a couple times, fortunately in nice weather, and he was able to correct with dead reckoning navigation, using some VOR frequencies and visual reference. But again, the course lies fed into the onboard equipment were way off, as though they were still experimenting with it, not able to fine-tune their numbers. They might not have even known they were doing it to us. Could have just been someone experimenting without realizing they were hooking onto our system.

"If they get it tweaked, my fear is they will be able to throw headings and approaches off by a degree or two, trip up the glideslope slightly or the heading by a fraction of a degree. Under certain circumstances, that small amount is all they would need to do damage. At some of our airports, it could be the difference between landing on a runway or an interstate."

"And, Matt," Dr. Halstead asked, "what's the difference whether it's off one degree, a half degree or 180 degrees?"

"Big difference, I'd say. The degree of precision makes it an entirely new ballgame."

"Oh," she said.

"Now I'm not one to go into the terrorist panic mode," Matt continued to the rest of the room, "but if someone wanted to be selective in terms of who they threw off course, they could create disasters at will."

"Be selective at one degree or 20 degrees," Halstead said. "I repeat, what's the difference?"

"Nineteen," a voice said. No one laughed.

"The problem is," Matt said, "if the terrorists keep their mouths shut and don't look for the publicity as they're wont to do, they can pick and choose with impunity what aircraft and ships to crash. Everyone will be screaming pilot error and absolutely no one will know it was a terrorist act. They wouldn't be looking for something like GPS problems in terms of vertical guidance or anything. It would just be an accident investigation, nothing more."

"Then it's *not* terrorism," Dr. Halstead said, bringing some forced laughter.

"Exactly," Matt said. "If it were terrorism, someone would be out there screaming radical stuff and taking credit. I say they aren't going to scream anything in the future. They'll just sit patiently and wait for their targets of opportunity. And that, of course, is where the danger lies. And believe me, it gets better. I mean worse. They can also hack into military frequencies, the ones that guide rockets, bombs and those sorts of things. They even stole the source code controlling satellite and missile guidance systems. The whole deal fit onto one floppy disk. Doesn't get much better than that for them, whoever *they* are."

"Really, Matt, come on," Dr. Halstead said. "You're overreacting. You know our military scrambles their nav signals and their guidance devices."

"Of course they do, but how about just one getting through—just one in 100? Their chances of success have increased exponentially. Before they had no shot. Now any ten-year-old cutting school can have access to more on the Internet than just how to make a pipe bomb. They can get in and play with the big boys and girls now. They might be playing it like a video game. Again, they might not even know they're on the airwaves screwing things up."

Pat Shepherd tapped Matt on the leg and handed him his cell phone. A buzzer sounded on Dr. Halstead's speakerphone at the front of the table.

"Anything in the articles about where these people are or who they are?" Dr. Halstead asked.

"I'd say any kid in any country with a computer, a GPS and a brain could pull this off," Matt said. "They're techno-entrepreneurs with an eye for business, and I am here to tell you that they have one expensive item to sell if it works. And it does work."

Dr. Halstead spoke quietly into the speakerphone beside her laptop and smoldering cigarette in the crystal ashtray. She flipped her phone closed.

"Well, this helps," she said. "Some cable people were working their lines in Pittsburgh. Seems they found three small antennae, one attached to a telephone pole and one behind a billboard on the west side of Interstate 279 leading into Pittsburgh International. There was another in the terminal building near the tower. The cable guys took the ones down on their poles. Wasn't any authorization for the things to be there, so they just tore 'em up. They didn't know what to do with the information, so they called Patricia at our Homeland Security office."

"Maybe they're collocated," Matt said. "That would sure solve the problem of closing the distance between transmissions and the target. But give them a little more time and they won't even need that collocated stuff. Just fly a private aircraft near an airliner and they have free rein."

Dr. Halstead took a long drag on her cigarette. "Maybe they should put them back up, try triangulating or something," she said.

"Oh, please," Matt said. "They could be transmitting now. Just what we need."

"Renee," Dr. Halstead said into the speakerphone. "Get me Ray Andre at DARPA." The Defense Advanced Research Projects Agency.

The large oak doors opened. A small man in khaki work clothes pushed a bucket on wheels into the room. He held a mop handle in place to keep it from falling out of the soapy water. He was old with white, slicked-back hair and a clean-shaven face. His left eye was glass, a light blue color. His right was hazel.

"*Przepraszam,* I'm sorry, good Doctor," he said, looking at Dr. Halstead.

"That's okay, Petrov. Come on in. We're done here. Go ahead and mop your brains out. *Dziekuje,* thank you," she said in her best, but not very good, Polish pronunciation. She was the only one who ever tried speaking some Polish to the man. He seemed to like it and besides, he kept her ashtrays clean and did anything she asked of him. There were jokes about it in the office. When they spoke of the two, it was orifice, not office.

People began filing out of the room.

"One minute," Wilhamena shouted. "Just one damn minute. None of you have been excused."

Petrov stood at attention beside the mop handle and bucket. He extended his chest and the buttons on his sweat-stained shirt pulled. Halstead looked at him and gestured to the doors. He remained at attention and rolled the bucket and mop to the hall. He grabbed the doors and pulled them closed.

Chatter was replaced with a bungling silence as the naughty employees took their assigned seats.

"Business as usual," Wilhamena said. "That's what we have here. We simply go on a heightened alert, redouble our security, be aware of what's going on around us and report anything out of the ordinary. We've been here before and we'll be here again. It is called life in the 21st century, my colleagues. Nothing substantive has happened and all we have here is conjecture, fear and techno-paranoia. However, I will take no chances of this institution going down the tubes on my watch. This meeting is adjourned. Open the door and let Petrov in. I want this room antiseptic. There's a lot of garbage to clear out of here."

14

Bertrum Randolph looked upon e-bombs as being no real challenge. They were electrically dirty blasts some governments were experimenting with that emitted a high-energy pulse of microwaves that could wreak the destruction of a lightning strike.

In addition, it could fry everything electrical in a particular area from toasters to computer chips, and it did not need to be on target like a dirty bomb. It could incinerate electronic ignitions in vehicles and aircraft. For Randolph's purposes, for the purposes of fun and profit, it needed to be done within a realm of subtle destruction, not a blatant blast for the public and governments to be aware of.

It was, in his mind, a simple matter of marketing, the same as anything in a store is marketed. Buy the e-bomb and choose where and when to launch a small aircraft or radar-controlled drone to ignite within e-bomb striking distance of an aircraft, ship or building. No one will know what caused the system failures in the target, especially if the detonation took place during a storm, Mother Nature's built-in camouflage.

Or you could not include that exact offering. The purchaser, the shopper in this case, might wish to go with the package that includes only the GPS dithering technology. And of course there is the matter of installation. Hell, you pay to have hot water heaters installed; how about something as big as an e-bomb or GPS scrambler?

Randolph & Associates will install for this price, or your people can install at no extra cost, or you may wish Randolph Inc.'s assistance at somewhat of a discount. Owner-assisted installation.

The best of both worlds to Bertrum was the Saturday night blue-light blue bomb special. "I'll build it, I'll launch it, I'll watch it all happen. Oh yes, and no checks. Cash only."

15

Sunny felt the vibration of the cell phone on her lap. She moved one of the earpieces of her headset to the side and pressed the phone to her ear. "Hello."

"Sunny, Matt here. Where are you now?"

There was a long silence. Matt heard the solid rumble of the 310-horsepower Continental engine in the background.

"Sunny, you there? Can you hear me?"

Sunny looked through the windshield of the Cirrus toward Pittsburgh. She saw the lights below her, the clear sky above and part of the Pittsburgh terminal disappearing into a black mass of weather. Allegheny County, her destination was directly in front of her. *Severe clear,* she thought.

"Just ready to land, Matt. What the hell happened to you? You hung up on me."

"I didn't," he said.

"When the phone goes dead, the party has hung up, Matt. What am I supposed to think?"

"I didn't hang up. Security hung up for me."

"I don't know about this long-distance relationship by phone. It's just—"

A voice crackling in Sunny's left earpiece halted her train of thought. "Cirrus approaching AGC, do you read?"

"Allegheny Tower, go ahead," she said.

"What? What did you say?" Matt asked.

Sunny put the phone down on the seat.

"You're cleared straight in, Cirrus. Got some real bad weather painting on the Doppler here. You want to get down now. It's coming in a lot faster than we thought."

"That's affirmative," Sunny said.

She picked up the cell phone. "Gotta' go. Landing ahead of weather," she said.

"You can call me back when you get down," Matt said.

Sunny looked at the lights of Allegheny County and the crimson, red and amber glow in the warm cockpit. "Yeah, I suppose I could." Click.

Guess it's just you and me for now, Clayton, she thought.

16

This is bullshit, Matt thought. *My job, my girl, damn coworkers who won't even acknowledge me. Rather bury their heads in the sand. Besides, I thought I quit, didn't I?*

Matt turned back to his already-open cell phone and punched in Butch Dominion's cell number.

"Butch Dominion, can I help you?"

"Butch, Matt Harmond here. Where are you?" Matt laughed out loud before Butch could respond.

"What's so funny, Mr. Harmond?"

"Nothing. Just seems I'm going around today checking on where people are. Doesn't seem to be doing me any good, though."

"Oh, I see."

"Uh, Butch, I need to schedule the Citation. You still anywhere near Atlantic City, maybe pick me up?"

"Mr. Harmond, this is unusual. I've never scheduled through anyone other than the admin people back at the Hughes Center." He paused, obviously thinking. "But, you know, well, that's fine—I suppose."

"When can you pick me up for a flight to Pittsburgh?"

"How about tomorrow, early?" Dominion asked.

"How about today, as soon as you can get to the airport?"

17

Captain Harding and First Officer Blaster looked at the glowing screen in front of them. "Cover that LAAS readout with a sticky or something, Duane. It's lying through its damn high-tech teeth."

"Worked last time," he said.

"Humor me," she said.

Her voice was mellow, hypnotic and not in the slightest bit flustered now. She didn't need to be transparent, or aware. In her mind, and apparently in her mind alone, she was fighting for her life.

First Officer Blaster was impressed with her calm under fire, but there was no way he was going to admit it.

"Don't hide them, damn it, use them," he said. "They're worth their weight in gold, especially in this turbulence and wind shear. These gauges are state of the art."

The approach speeds fluctuated up and down and Captain Harding fought to keep her ship on what she believed was the correct course. That heading, however, was up for debate according to Blaster.

Duane was surprised at how panicked his voice sounded. He'd never heard it like this in all his years of piloting large transport aircraft. *It's her damn pseudo calmness, Miss In-Charge.* Thoughts rushed through his mind in a slow motion jumble of images and close calls he'd had over years of flying. Yet nothing matched his current situation. *She's incompetent,* he thought. *She's pretending she's calm. She's delusional. I have to do something to save us. Us, hell, save myself! Shit, she's going to calmly plaster me all over the Pittsburgh countryside!*

18

The knock at the door was loud. A voice screamed above the wail of the wind blowing through the small cracks in Bertrum Randolph's window frames. He checked the plastic he had thrown over the backs of his computers as a precaution against the moisture. His second-floor apartment above the deli was no Ritz suite.

"Dr. Randolph, I have your coleslaw and fish here. Are you there?"

"Slide it under the door. I'll come down and pay later. I'm busy."

"It won't fit under the door, asshole. And you already owe us $54.98. If I don't get it now, you don't get the fish and slaw."

"I'm so very sorry," he said. "Hang on, let me open the door. I have some change here, maybe a tip in this for your trouble."

"Wow, another tip, Dr. Randolph?" the young female voice retorted, heavy on sarcasm. "I'll be able to pay my first semester at Pitt if you give me another 50 cents like last time."

"Smart-ass kids," Randolph said quietly so as not to be heard through the door. "They're all alike. Don't know the value of a buck anymore."

"You want the fish or not?" the delivery girl asked, growing impatient.

"I have some problems here right now," he said. "This storm is killing me. Stuff isn't working."

"I'll leave the slaw outside the door. But if you want the fish, you have to pay now. Come on, man, you got the bucks. You never go anywhere. Save money on dates, don't you?"

Randolph opened the door gently.

"Here's some money," he said to the emaciated girl. She had what he called nose armor piercing both nostrils. He leaned closer to her when he spoke and studied the two studded, stainless piercings through her tongue, one near the tip and one to the back of her tongue where it surely would interfere with swallowing. God only knows what she swallowed and what she did with those filthy things.

"I have dates," he said to her. "You just don't see me. How old are you, anyway?"

"Not old enough to date you, Pops."

"Why do you pierce your pretty little body?"

"I have piercings you could only dream of, Dr. Randolph. Just give me the money, please."

He reached into both of his pockets and pulled out a collection of coins.

"Here, hold out your hands."

"Please," she said. "Not again."

"It is legal tender. Now give me my fish."

She took the change and stuck it in her black apron. It weighted the apron and skirt down in the front, exposing some belly button piercings.

He pointed at them.

"Do they hurt? May I touch them?"

"Back off, Doc. You're a bit too close for comfort. No, they don't hurt unless someone tugs on them. Hey, I'm into computers. Look at that stuff. What do you have going on here?"

She started into his room. The plastic curtains on the windows moved with the rhythm of the wind streaking through the cracks.

"What the hell," she said. "You into model airplanes, are you? That thing is big. You build it yourself?"

Randolph put his hand on her chest and pushed her out of the room.

"Watch it, old man," she yelled. "Keep your fucking hands off me! Touch me again and I'll rip your little balls off."

"Hey, girl. You ought to go to Carnegie Mellon. You don't fit into Pitt—a mouth like that," he said. "And you come in here again and there will be no more tips."

He saw her flipping him the finger as he slammed the door in her face. He sat down and smelled the fish. He looked at the screens in front of him and instantly saw the disconnect that could only have been caused by a major power failure or an antenna problem. The power was okay, even though the storm outside was still raging.

Piss on the antennas, he thought. *Storm probably took one of them out. Maybe it's radio control e-bomb time. God, I love this life.*

19

Sunny scanned her instruments even though she was in perfectly clear weather for the moment. Her weather radar painted her in the clear, but within close proximity to the convective activity approaching her.

It was one of those scenarios inexperienced pilots got suckered into. They saw clear weather in front of them and continued on their course, believing they could get out if any serious activity presented a problem. They finally looked behind them and realized as the weather closed in, they had no way out of it since the stuff behind them closed in without them knowing it. They then found themselves in a common accident scenario—visual flight rules into instrument meteorological conditions. In other words, they couldn't see outside the airplane and they didn't have the experience or equipment to deal with it.

Sunny felt confident flying her Cirrus, which was loaded with nearly the same equipment that commercial airline pilots had at their fingertips.

Below her in the storm-covered Strip District of Pittsburgh, a man finished his coleslaw and left the last bite of fish sandwich for the cat. He noticed his collocated antennae weren't working and walked over to his model aircraft, the one with a Playboy bunny painted on the vertical stabilizer.

20

A radio-controlled aircraft buff since high school, Randolph watched the harmless hobby turn into a technically satisfying avocation. Not only was it satisfying, it was part of his marketing strategy, the backup for a problem such as antenna failure or software glitches that, unlikely as it might be, could happen to his equipment.

Price would of course be affected, he theorized. But the job, or at least most of the job, could still be completed in a more primitive fashion. And of course, good marketing man that he was, the price would be lowered if the customer had to resort to backup equipment. Such is war.

Range was no longer a problem for him in terms of getting a very small e-bomb onboard his radio-controlled model. Or better yet, depending on the size of the job, models. One model, ten models, 25, what did it matter? The e-bomb blast capability would multiply greatly with the addition of more flights.

He knew that in August 2003, after numerous failures, a model aircraft launched by some radio-controlled aircraft buffs successfully flew from Canada to County Galloway, Ireland. The entire flight took 38 hours and covered just a little less than 2,000 miles. A miniature Lindbergh accomplishment. The balsa wood and Mylar model used satellite navigation and an autopilot system and was controlled by engineers and radio operators using laptops not unlike Dr. Randolph's.

To Randolph the simplicity of that flight was beautiful. The aircraft was powered with camping lantern fuel, and although technicians controlling the flight lost contact with the model for nearly three hours, the record-breaking flight was completed safely.

In comparison to the difficulties faced by the transatlantic flight of the model plane, Dr. Randolph's proximity to Pittsburgh International and any other number of high-density airports was a piece of cake.

Hell with the cat, he thought, popping the last piece of cold fish into his mouth as he opened his apartment door, the black radio-controlled aircraft held gently in his arms.

He swore when he banged the port wing of the aircraft into the wall as he turned to negotiate the steps down to the deli area.

"Dr. Randolph, where are you going with that thing in this weather?" It was the pierced girl leaning against the wall under an awning, sucking her tobacco stick.

He turned toward her. "Will you please hold this door for me and get these damned customers out of my way!"

21

Randolph leaned the aircraft in the backseat of his van and placed the radio control apparatus on the floor. He took I-279 to US 22/30 to PA 60, then Exit 6 to the airport. He looked for his second antenna, the one on the carwash bulletin board at Exit 3. It wasn't there.

The antennae were not attached securely, the way he would normally do it. The first one on the roof of his Strip District apartment was anchored with metal bands to the chimney. But the remaining placements were leaned, stuck, wedged and anchored in whatever way he could quickly find to keep them in place, the location being much more important than the attachment hardware itself.

He pulled into the airport complex, scanning the parking lot paralleling the Landside Terminal. Weather was forecasted to clear and the lot was filling. He stopped and pulled out the model, fondling it in his hands for a brief moment. This place was too crowded. He'd be seen in a minute. He shoved the radio-controlled model back into the van and slid into the driver's seat.

Not today. Plus I don't need no stinking model airplane. I'll try Allegheny County. Less traffic, less congestion, maybe excellent reception when the storm clears. Just a test. Who gives a shit?

22

In the distance toward PIT, Sunny saw the lightning but no thunder, the headset and engine noise drowning any audio of the storm. She received her clearance from Allegheny Tower and landed.

The old airport was deserted. Joyco Air was putting in its last corporate jet before the storm hit. The crew looked toward PIT as they pushed the button igniting the hydraulics that closed the massive hangar door.

Sunny opened the Cirrus door and felt a rush of air blow into the cockpit. She looked around for an ambulance, a hearse, anything to extract and carry her dead cargo to its final resting place.

She looked out into a parking lot with a few cars there, probably the tower crew and a custodian. She tied the Cirrus down and tugged at the ropes. She repeatedly brushed her hair out of her face, but the wind kept smacking it around. She walked through the airport lounge and out the back door of the rundown facility. She saw a bar across the street and decided to use the phone, maybe grab a drink or two. She wouldn't be flying east this night. Storms tracked east and that wasn't where she wanted to be.

Sunny didn't lock the door of the Cirrus, but that wasn't unusual. Her grandfather had taught her not to lock it. "Makes it easy for them to get into the plane," he'd say. They're going to get in anyhow. This way you won't have a door to replace one way or the other, if some thief in the night wanted into your aircraft to lift some very expensive electronics—or corpses—you may as well let them in. You could save the expense of a door if the dummies knew enough to try opening it before they broke in.

It was much cheaper that way. Replacing doors, latches, locks or broken windows tended to be expensive. He'd shown her where to leave some old credit cards and a few bucks in a wallet as a decoy. Cut your losses.

Besides, she thought, *who is going to crawl over a dead body to steal a few bucks? It's better than having a guard dog.*

23

Trog Svladen walked into the Allegheny Airport Bar and Restaurant like he was walking onto a stage. His cigarette was pinched between the middle and ring fingers of his right hand. He sat at a barstool in front of a mirror that covered all 20 feet of the wall behind the bar. He chose a seat beside a blonde with heavy makeup, tight red leather pants and an umbrella drink like it was the Keys rather than rainy Pittsburgh. Her ashtray was full of cigarettes with bright red lipstick rings around them. An empty pack was crumpled in the ashtray. Her lighter was sitting by her purse. Printed on it in bright orange letters were the words, "My Fucking Lighter."

"*Dobry wieczor,*" he said to the lady in red, simultaneously putting a $50 bill on the bar.

"Pardon me?" she said.

"My country it mean good evening," he said.

"Oh," she said. "And to you too."

He and the blonde were the only two at the bar. There were three women and two men sitting at a booth in the northeast corner of the dining area that looked out onto one of the AGC runways. The restaurant was separated from the bar by a three-foot-high divider with artificial plants on top. The plants needed dusting. For some reason there was a swinging gate in the middle of the fence.

Svladen slid the bill toward the bartender.

"Michelob Ultra. Large if it be on draft."

"We do," the bartender said. "Twenty ounces okay?"

"Better than other sixteen."

He looked over at the blonde. She was swizzling the umbrella, mixing her drink. He tapped his finger on the bar.

"They going to have celebrate for us," he said. "Give award for sticking to our diets, only drinking little bit. Aren't they?"

"Pardon me?" the blonde said.

Her words were slow, over pronounced like she had to work at making herself understood, the way people speak loudly and succinctly when trying to get a child to understand. She uncrossed her legs, turned her barstool toward him and crossed them again.

"Just kidding to you. Sorry," he said. "Try to make conversation. Kill time. You watch your weight, take care of yourself. You lift the weights?"

"Really, buddy, you must be kidding. That's it? That's the line? Please, either quit or try again. Your lines must be from the old country. We've advanced a bit more here, but actually, maybe not that much. I've had worse."

"You mean there chance for me and you?" he asked.

"Not really. Talk, yeah. But that's all. What are you doing here? Where you from?"

"Waiting for someone," he said. "No, waiting for two people. One live and one dead."

"You're not serious, are you? I mean, it's a joke. Not a funny joke, but a joke. Maybe a European joke. Continental?"

"I am Polish," he said. "No joke. It is my job. Proud Polish."

"Really?" she asked.

"No," he said. "I'm joke with you, lady. Really, I'm not Polish, and this accent, although fairly convincing, is far from being real. I'm no more from Poland than you're a nun just looking for a quick drink on your way back to the convent. But I must tell you I like to think of myself as a modern-day Samurai. Not like a Jap or anything like that, but a today kind of a warrior, a contemporary. You know what I'm saying to you? I don't lop off heads like they did. I'm Americanized, civilized."

The blonde downed the rest of her drink and pushed it toward the bartender.

"Another?" the bartender asked.

"Let me get that for you." Trog shoved another $50 at the bartender, making certain the lady saw he had more than one.

"Warriors, Samurais especially, have a different sense of death and life. They're beyond such things. Ya know lady, warriors will cut their horses' throats and drink the blood, then sew it back up when they're done with their little drinky-pooh. Just like a mother would sew a hole in your sweater. Sometimes they have to gut it and climb inside if they need the warmth. I mean if they really need to. That's the point. They don't kill unless it's needed."

He fingered through the bills in his wallet. The lady was left speechless by his choice of topic.

"I hate hundreds in the wallet," he said and tapped his fingers on the bar. "I keep them in the money clip. I like organizing like that. I get mixed up sometimes. Hundreds in pocket, fifties in wallet. I forget things. Maybe that's better. I don't know. Sometimes you need to forget some things. You hear me, lady? I said, do you hear me?"

She shook her head and re-crossed her legs, still not sure what to say.

"Oh, I see," he said. "Red leather pants. Those real?"

He reached over and touched her left knee.

"Yeah, they're real. Two legs, crotch," she said.

"Oh, crotch," he said.

"Yeah."

"I thought you said you weren't interested."

"That's before I knew you had hundreds in your pants and fifties in your wallet."

"That's not all I have in my pants, lady."

"Well, Mr. Whatever-Your-Name-Is. What do you do for fun? Read much? Maybe subscribe to *Guns, Ammo & Incendiary Devices*?"

"Sort of, but mostly knives. I like knives. Samurai sword can cost $85,000."

"Buddy," she said, "I don't know about this. I get the feeling you have a dark side."

"What side would you like to see?"

Svladen lightly placed his index fingers on her knees. He gently pushed them open then closed.

"Gee, they have real nice action like a well-lubricated machine. Doesn't seem to take much to move them."

She turned away, faced the mirror and finished the umbrella drink.

"Maybe next time," she said. "I hardly know you."

"Sure, but I don't know if I'll ever be back here after I'm done. Wanna go to church or something religious first?" he asked. "Christ wasn't perfect. And we're learning a lot about stuff they didn't tell us when we were kids going to Sunday school. I read where early Christians hid some gospels from us, but I get a magazine that tells me the truth. Keeps me up on this stuff. In the know."

"What do you keep in your other pockets?" she said.

He laughed and patted her on the back as she stuck her personalized lighter in her purse.

"Oh, look," he said. "It's security."

A uniformed old man pulled up one of the stools at the end of the bar and sat down.

"A cold one, please. My off-duty reward," the old guy said to the bartender.

"Uniforms, I never did understand them," Svladen said. "Like parades. What's the point?"

He leaned over and whispered into Red Leather's ear. "Do you know what a uniform means? You know what a uniform is, lady? Nazis wore uniforms. Nice ones, too. This old guy needs a lesson from the Nazis. But I got business to tend to. I'm finished with you for now. Maybe I'll see you later."

"Oh, you are a true sweetheart," she said as she stirred her tropical drink.

24

Svladen lit another cigarette and walked out of the bar. The cigarette dangled from his mouth. He stuck the fingers of both hands through the interlocking wire spaces in the Cyclone fence surrounding the aircraft tie-down area. He watched Sunny walk to the bar. He moved toward the opening she was going to have to pass through in order to get to the bar entrance.

"May I help you, ma'am?" Trog Svladen said in perfect English.

"No thanks. Cell phone battery went dead. Using the bar phone. And, uh, you are?"

"Just work here, little missy. I'm security. No wife and kids to go home to. Nice Cirrus. Don't see many of those around here."

He took his hands from the fence and dragged heavily on his cigarette.

"Can't be too careful. Let me walk you to the bar. Could be crazies around here. Never know. You wouldn't believe what I see."

Sunny said, "No thanks."

"As you wish, young lady. As you wish. Got some weather moving in real soon, aye? You have a good evening. If you're here tomorrow, I'll look for you at the fuel farm. You take care now, hear?"

"Yeah," Sunny said. "Bye."

The man flipped his cigarette over the top of the fence toward the plane and watched Sunny go into the bar as he headed for the Cirrus and Clayton Meadows. Lightning lit up the Pittsburgh skyline.

He looked up into the tower area. There were no signs of controllers, no one peering into the quiet night, no air traffic at AGC in anticipation of the storm headed from PIT. Lights reflected off the windows.

He walked toward Sunny's Cirrus, watching the tower to be sure they didn't have a clear view of him and the SR22. He jumped onto the wing and stuck a three-foot-long probe through the slight crack between the copilot's side door and the fuselage of the aircraft, not checking to see if it had been left unlocked. There was a loud popping sound when he forced the door open at the latch point. Some shards of paint and debris shot into the cabin and landed on the transport bag.

He kneeled on both knees and leaned into the cockpit. He smelled the sweet scent of Sunny's lingering perfume and the pungent solvent. He patted Meadows on the foot.

"Hmmm," he said to the bag. "Sweet lingering scent of a lady."

He placed himself on top of the corpse, his face directly over the area the corpse's face should be, about the size of a chicken. He stretched into the back and undid the straps securing the prone passenger.

He slithered off Meadows and knelt back down onto the wing, slapped both of his hands onto either side of the bag and tugged the dead weight out onto the wing. He took a deep breath and turned his head to the tower.

There were red lights and shadows but no air traffic controllers looking out onto an empty runway. The area was abandoned except for a few cars, a Chevy S10 and a red Toyota Sequoia SUV. He heard heavy metal departing Pittsburgh International, its navigation lights climbing into the hot summer sky.

He saw the rear entrance of the Allegheny Bar. There was a small dumpster, a light suspended above it, a wooden screen door with some holes in it and the muffled sounds of a television news station, maybe a weather channel. He thought about the lady in the red leather pants. He swore and kept tugging at the stubborn bag.

He wrapped his arms around the bottom of the bag and squeezed it to his chest. He pulled it off the wing. "Ouch," he said when the head hit the pavement. He turned around with his prize package in tow and trolled toward the Sequoia, leaning forward like he was angled into a gale-force wind, struggling to make a few inches of ground.

"Fucking corpse sinner," he said, then crossed himself and repeated, "Forgive me, my Lord, for I have sinned. My last confession was, ah, I forget. Piss on it."

He was sweating and didn't like it and he didn't want to turn the air on full blast in the SUV because it would give him a cold, make him weak, less than the man he could be. And he couldn't stand that.

If he had a corn on his foot, a slight sprain, an ingrown hair, he didn't feel right because he was then imperfect. He was only partial, fragmented and not the way God intended him to be.

He occupied his mind and mumbled as he dragged his prize, practicing. "*Mi casa es su casa, es muy importante bien, dzien dobry*. How do you do, ma'am? I'm the director of maintenance, Dobranoc, may I give you a ride? I find you attractive."

He had rules and one was like the U.S. Army commercial where you can "Be all you can be," and if that wasn't to be, then he considered himself defective. What possible use would he be? Be one, be many, be well.

He had a washer and dryer, and an expensive iron that steamed and made hissing noises when he placed it upright. He would press his underwear, T-shirts and jeans and if he felt up to it, sheets and pillowcases as he'd stand there practicing dialect.

After the body was stashed in the SUV, he rested in the driver's seat, sweating, his head resting on the steering wheel. He raised it and smashed it down two times. When he struck it for the second time, a small red splotch of blood remained on the wheel. He sat up, took a deep breath and cried wet, childlike sobs.

"I hate colds," he said to the corpse in the back. "I will get a cold. I hate it."

Svladen flipped open his cell phone and pushed auto-dial. He dabbed the red from his forehead and took out his handkerchief to clean up the mess while he waited. A voice answered, "Yes?"

"Me here with the package," he said.

"The girl see you?"

"Well, I guess, but no big shake. Right?"

"She needs to know not to remember you. That's all. Besides, aren't you the master of disguise?"

"Yeah, but sometimes I forget who I am to whom, or is it who?" he said. "I mean, one time I'm in a bar and I'm Latino, maybe a little bit of artificial sun rubbed on my face. Then I go in the bathroom and come out a cracker, white as a sheet."

"Well, whoever you were—are—she needs to know to forget about you. I'll get back to you if it has to go further than that. Listen, don't freelance with her and keep the package until I get back with you."

He reached into the breast pocket of his shirt, took out the handkerchief and rubbed the steering wheel. "Oh, I want to make her forget me," he said. "She's cute. I'd like that. Maybe I could be a Polish matador when I nail her."

"Just have a nice talk with her for now," the phone voice said.

Svladen snapped the cell phone closed and adjusted the seat to the recline position and waited.

Sunny came out of the bar and looked at the Cirrus tied down on the ramp. The wings were moving slightly in the gusts. Svladen heard the sound of a slamming door from the bar area. He pushed the up-button on the seat and waited until he could identify Sunny.

"Hey, you dropped this when you got out of your plane," he said. "Wind must have blown it over here."

He waved his hand in the shadowed darkness of the lonely airport parking lot. She looked and couldn't make out exactly what it was he was trying to show her.

"I don't know what it is. Looks complicated to me," he said. "I don't know anything about flying gadgets."

"One second," Sunny said as she headed toward the Sequoia.

She reached up to take the object out of his hand at the same time he pushed open the door. It hit her solidly on the right hand. She heard a cracking noise and reached for her thumb. She felt cold metal on her neck and a dizzying electrical shock, then darkness. There was a woozy feeling like she was going to throw up as she felt her left knee hit the pavement. The last thing she remembered was the slick feeling of the body bag beneath her. She couldn't move.

Before complete darkness took over, she heard something. It was the sound of her voice. It sounded like a prayer.

25

First she felt a stinging on her neck, a burning soreness when she tried to find consciousness in the murky black of her mind. She reached for her neck and couldn't feel her arms move. Her eyes wouldn't open. She willed it to happen. She willed it over and over until first the right then left eye opened and saw a blur of light and color, a sort of mauve with speckles and dots. She shook her head and the dots went away for a while then came back. She heard sounds: a baseball announcer, a Pepsi commercial. She turned her head toward the noise and saw the flickering of a television. She tried to move her feet and couldn't. She felt cold and tilted her head down and saw that she was naked. She pressed her head down as far as it could go and saw the gold cross and chain shining between her breasts. Duct tape bound her hands and feet.

As her vision cleared she saw a man sitting in a chair beside the television watching her. She could not make out his face in the shadows.

"Don't you be scared for you," he said. "I not hurt. You just listen what I say."

She listened, didn't speak.

"You story is you lost the body in the plane. Went in bar and come out and gone. Maybe kids take it. Pitt fraternity prank or someting. You say noting, you be fine. Play it down. Must play it down."

The room was clear in her eyes now. She looked at the generic wallpaper, compressed sawdust furniture, small signs on the walls and door probably explaining checkout time and room service numbers. Cheap motel room.

I hate Matt, she thought.

"You a lucky lady, miss. I not steal your kidneys and sell for forty thousand each. Big market," he said.

She squirmed and watched the short man stand up and walk over to her. He stood inches from her naked body and looked up and down the long, sleekness of it.

Today his hair was white and slicked back, shining in the fluorescent motel light suspended above Sunny. He pushed his hair back then rubbed his hands together, lathering them up with whatever oil he had used.

He turned around and walked over to the door, opened it, stood back from the hallway and looked down the hall. There was the smell of stale tobacco and cigar smoke mixed with disinfectant. He saw no one in the hall. He walked back into the room and placed the motel phone beside her head and took it off the hook.

"You can get to this if squirm," he said. "Call the 911. They be here and you still have kidneys and liver in you. More than I can say for last one."

He went into the bathroom, took off the slicked-back white hair, splashed some water on his long brown hair and towel-dried it. He took a tube of adhesive and a brown mustache from his pocket and dabbed it securely onto his upper lip. He walked out of the bathroom with his face toward the hallway wall, keeping it away from Sunny's view. He went into the hallway, closed the door and cleared his throat.

"Me, me, me, me, me," he said to himself "Practice, practice, practice. Hi, how ya'll doin'? In the market for any Western wear? Got some good hats in my vehicle, by golly. Wanna check 'em out? Stetsons. Good price."

26

The first thing Sunny did when Matt saw her at the police station was slap him across the face. Then she kicked him in the shins, first the left then right.

He reached down and grabbed one, then felt the pain in the other. "Oh, man," he said. "Stop."

"Never on God's green earth would this have happened if you would just get unmarried to your job," she said. "What a weekend, Matt."

"I got here, didn't I?" he said. "I mean, what else do you want? What can I do? Just tell me. I got here at jet speed."

The state police barracks was in a converted ranch house, lockers and showers in the basement. The upstairs was organized with movable dividing walls that could be rolled between desks. They were supposed to be acoustically treated for noise attenuation, but you could make out just about every word said on the first floor, except the unisex bathroom—you could hear the flush, but not much more.

Two female troopers and one male trooper watched as Sunny wound up to slap Matt again. Smiling, they looked at her and shook their heads. Sunny put down her right hand and said to Matt, "You really do make me mad. I don't want anything to do with you."

Matt reached into his pocket and handed her a handkerchief.

"Keep it," she said. "You'll not see me cry."

27

Pittsburgh from the air at night was a kaleidoscope of color, warmth and beauty. With cold front passage processing through the Pittsburgh area, it was made more dramatic. There were random appearances of lights, then shrouded darkness as cloud cover blanketed the ground. After frontal passage there would be pure, clean, clear skies—nature's cleansing of the atmosphere.

For now, nothing was pure or clean for Captain Lorraine Harding and First Officer Duane Carlson Blaster in the front office of their Boeing 767-300 Freighter.

First Officer Blaster did not know how they had arrived at their current position, but as black clouds and ground fog cleared for a fraction of a second, the Pittsburgh International Airport came into view. According to his calculations, they weren't supposed to be where they were. The instruments had in fact lied.

Everything Blaster had told Captain Harding had been wrong. The instruments were not telling the truth and *her* instincts were correct. She had found the airport through the use of instinct, compass headings and an old-fashioned VOR navigational aid that fortunately worked on different frequencies than GPS signals.

The problem remaining was their unusually steep angle of a pitch down attitude and the placement of the runways. Captain Harding was not set up for the approach and had descended below the overcast. Climbing back into the clouds and rain with instruments that lied was not a good idea.

Which ones did you trust? They would be back at square one with nowhere to go. *Just another guessing game*, Captain Harding thought.

"Boeing 767 Heavy approaching PIT," the controller's voice said. "Your speed is up and you're not on the localizer, Captain. Headed for the mall, not the runway. Is there a problem? Would you like to declare an emergency, a missed approach?"

"PIT Approach, Heavy here. Stand by, please," she said.

"Duane, I don't think we're going to have the spool time to wind this thing up for a go around. I'm going to land it. I have to land it."

She keyed the push to talk switch. "PIT, Heavy here. Not declaring at this time," she said.

"For the love of God, Harding," the first officer said. "This is no Piper Cub. You can't make that runway. No way."

"Hey, Blaster," she said in a monotone voice, still concentrating on flying the airplane. "If I'd have listened to you, we'd be planted in Heinz Field about now."

Pilots in general, and captains in charge of ships of any kind, do not usually wish to declare emergencies. For all the wrong reasons, it's like admitting that you (the one in charge) have done something wrong. You (the one in charge) could have and should have taken care of this problem when you saw it developing because emergencies usually don't just happen; they are sequential. One bad or worrisome thing happens and then a second, then you say to yourself, *We still should be okay*. But you aren't. It is the captain of the *Titanic* and others who, in the best and worst hours of their command, made decisions based on ego.

Harding was a skilled pilot, but she couldn't help wonder if she was making the right decisions.

Dark clouds and the blur of cockpit lights and the lights of the city combined to create a dreamlike aura. Sight-bites of photos flashed through Captain Harding's head as she fought the controls of the huge aircraft. The players in her mind appeared in slow motion. The cloud cover lifted for one, two seconds, teasing her before wrapping the 767 in blackness.

More pictures flashed through her head: Saturday morning breakfasts, kids at the beach, the dog jumping up on the bed. She saw the bright blonde strands of her son's hair. *Why the hair?* she thought. And then his Bermuda shorts, the ones with the big cargo pockets, the ones he liked to call "commando pants."

"Duane, get a grip," Harding said. "It is our only chance. We don't know what will quit working next."

For the first time, Blaster sat in the copilot's seat, his mouth shut while he handled radios, fumbled through electronic checklists intermittently looking outside at clouds, lights, blackness and bubbles of moisture sweeping their horizontal trails across the windscreen. He made no sexist comments.

Harding pushed hard left rudder then forward on the yoke, forcing the nose down below what she knew was a critical angle.

"Give me a hand with the rudder, Duane, will you?"

"Sure, Captain," he said. "Whatever I can do to help."

In all the controlled confusion of GPS failings and navigation problems, she couldn't help but glance over at her first officer. To her amazement, he was hard at work doing those things first officers do for their captains.

She was startled by bursts of turbulence back into her tunnel of concentration, a concentration needed desperately to survive.

28

"If it wasn't for the anonymous phone call to the state cops," Sunny said, "I'd still be tied to that bed waiting for my absentee hero on a white horse to rescue me."

"They didn't hurt you, did they? What did they want? What did they do to you?"

"A prank or something," Sunny said. "Medical students, I think—the way they sounded."

"I'm here, Sunny, for better or worse. And I know it seems worse," Matt said.

"I am history, Mr. GPS. I'm done. Can't deal with you anymore and just because of that realization, I'm feeling better already."

Sunny pushed through the metal and glass double doors leading to the sidewalk outside the state police ranch house barracks. Matt followed her, a bad boy lap dog in tow.

"The corpse was more company than you," she said.

"By the way," Matt said. "Where is the stiff?"

"Don't say stiff to me, you son of a bitch."

"I love when you talk sweet to me."

The female officer motioned to them. "Car's out there," she said.

Sunny and Matt got into the back of the state police car.

"This smells like the back seat of a state police car," Matt said.

He looked up at the broad shoulders of the female police officer sliding in behind the wheel.

"Work out, do you, Officer?" he asked.

"Where you guys want me to drop you? I'm going down to the Greyhound Terminal."

"Strip District would be good," Matt said.

Sunny tightened her seatbelt.

"Allegheny County Airport would be better for me. I can skirt around this storm. I'm going home."

"And don't call my unit smelly," the officer said.

Matt reached over to hold Sunny's left hand and she jerked it away before he got near.

"Please, come with me to the Strip," he said.

"You are quite the boy, Matt. Yes you are. Now I have an offer from an unemployed tech to have some fun in Pittsburgh. Just keeps getting better and better. And it's none of your business where the corpse is."

"Well," the state lady said, "we do need Mr. Meadows, ma'am. No body, no forensics. And without the corpse, they don't have a case against that bastard who ran him down off the coast of Cape May."

Sunny crossed her arms in a defiant gesture. "Take me to the airport. I'm going home to my condo. I have a right."

"Sorry, but you're going to have to stay here for a while, Ms. Patronski. I'm taking you to the airport to get your suitcase and I'll be dusting your plane for prints. That's what I do. I dust. Well, I just want to get your plane to a hangar. We have one out there with our chopper. Don't want those flyboys doing it, though. They'll take great care of your plane but will undoubtedly bastardize any prints I might get. So you'll be here awhile. Hope you like Pittsburgh."

As the police cruiser pulled out of the parking lot, Matt leaned over to Sunny. "Come with me to the Strip. I have a lead on who is doing the GPS dithering. I'll need your help. Pat Shepherd's flying in tomorrow, too. No, driving. You have me all messed up, Sunny. Boss doesn't know. No one knows but the three of us. I can solve this thing. I know I can."

"Dither me this," she said. "Why would I go? You find the person doing this, get asked to come back, get a promotion by that cradle-robbing boss of yours, then put in twice the hours you already do. So let's see, we can spend a few minutes a week together between your work dates with your computers and technicians. I don't think so."

The cruiser passed the deserted parking lot at Allegheny County, turned right behind the tower and went down a ramp to the state police chopper hangar. It was a rundown building constructed during World War II. The interior was immaculate with a battleship gray paint covering the floor, walls and raftered ceiling. A man in a long-sleeved khaki shirt and pants stopped pushing a broom when the state police car drove onto his clean gray floor.

"Hold it right there, Officer," he said. "Not one more inch onto this property." He put his hand up in a stop motion like a patrol boy outside an elementary school. He walked up to the driver, dragging his push broom behind him.

"Get out of here," he ordered the officer. He pointed to the tracks the cruiser had made. "Just look at this," he said. His voice was high, squeaky, like a middle-school California girl. "See those tracks. This place is spotless and it will stay that way or you will have to park in the lot and walk down."

"I need to put a plane in here tonight," the large state police lady said. "And I need to dust it."

"There will be no dusting in here. Just have a look around. It shines and that is only because of me and my rules."

The officer reached into the cruiser and pulled out the microphone. She turned away from the cleanliness nut and spoke a few sentences into the mike. She handed it to the man with the broom.

"Hello," he said.

He nodded his head up and down but said nothing as though the person on the other end of the airwaves could see him.

"Oh, yes, for sure, sir," he said. "Not a problem. Right away."

The custodian of cleanliness handed the officer her mike and said to her, loudly, "Put your car over there." He pointed at a neatly painted yellow rectangle outside on the north end of the hangar. "And stay in the yellow area. You don't, and one of the planes taxiing by is going to hit you with a wingtip or prop. Stay in the middle."

"Sir, yes, sir," the officer said sarcastically.

Mr. Clean put the broom on the floor and pulled a grease rag from his rear pocket and rubbed the wet tire tracks that had been made by the cruiser.

"Asshole cops," he mumbled.

Once the cruiser had parked in the epicenter dead middle of the yellow warning area, Sunny, Matt and the trooper got out and walked to the back of the hangar to the office area. As they got closer, they saw two uniformed state police officers and a man in a navy blue blazer, red tie and white button-down dress shirt. The man in the blazer opened the door and said, "Come on in." The custodian, holding a yellow plastic bucket, headed toward the wet footprints made by his guests.

Names, introductions, ranks, titles and a few laughs were exchanged among the group. Sunny handed the man in the blazer a set of keys to the Cirrus and she and Matt walked out into the hangar.

"Want to stay together till you can go home?" he asked. "I mean, maybe a nice bed and breakfast, like the Pritorian on Maple?"

"Same place, separate rooms," she said. "Best I can do. Maybe the innkeeper will be cute. Might even have time for a dinner date, some gourmet."

"Fine, just don't give up on me completely," Matt said. "And one more thing. Would you come with me to the 300 block in the Strip District first? I think I need to snoop around a bit. Well, maybe a lot."

They both turned toward the Rent-A-Wreck sign next to the hangar.

"Oh, Sunny," he said. "You have any money? I'm a little short."

29

Pat Shepherd opened the sunroof of his Audi Quattro to let in some fresh air. He struggled to dig some change and ones out of his pocket for the tollbooth. He'd driven for seven hours after receiving the call from Matt about his lead on the GPS pranksters or entrepreneurs or terrorists or whatever they were.

He paid the toll and punched the OnStar navigation button. The jazz station that had been playing on the radio was cut off by a pleasant female voice. "Yes, Mr. Shepherd, how may I help you?"

"I want to go to some inn in Pittsburgh—uh, The Priority, maybe The Priory, The Primavera. I'm not sure. Ethnic sounding."

"Thank you, Mr. Shepherd, I'll check out some names for you to choose from. Will that be of help?"

"Yes, please. Thanks. Which way do I go off the turnpike?"

"Let's see, I have you on the screen. You're getting off Exit 6 at Monroeville now?"

"Yeah, that's me."

"Mr. Shepherd, you don't have to shout. Just speak in a normal tone of voice. I see you've just signed on with us."

"Yes, new car. Just getting used to all this stuff on it."

While the OnStar service center looked up the bed and breakfast, Shepherd picked up his cellular from the passenger's seat and dialed Matt's number. Matt answered.

"Where are you?"

"On my way to the Strip with Sunny."

"How'd it go?"

"Tell you later, but she'll be with me at the location I triangulated. I mean, it's narrowed down. I'm not used to this stuff."

"So where you want me, Matt?"

"Head toward the Strip. Call me when you get there. You have a gun or a club or something?" Matt asked.

"Please, Matt. A club? I'm much more advanced. Besides, I don't think we're getting into a real big-time criminal element here. Maybe I'll pick up a club on the way. Really, buddy. Lighten up. Been watching too many cop movies."

Matt looked at street signs and tried to drive without making too many wrong turns.

"What are we looking for?" Sunny asked.

"An antenna, maybe more. Probably more. Also looking for the 300 block. It's going to be an educated guess. It's 300 to 340 Bramington. I can't get closer than that. Has to be something there to give us a lead."

"You are such a good date, Matt. And you know how to have fun. Antenna, huh?"

They parked across the street from the indicated address.

"Look, Sunny. The antenna. On the porch roof, just outside the window of that apartment above the deli. Check it out. Over there too, a collinear vertical, a stacked tuned dipole antenna system and a satellite radio antenna. Looks harmless enough. Who would ever guess? Just some radio junkie? Wrong."

"You mean it's this simple, Matt? Find some antennas and find the GPS thief in the night just because you think you're close?"

"Maybe," Matt said. "It is simple and that's the beauty and the ugliness of it. GPS receivers are vulnerable. It's been long known and no one cared until the government got involved in NAVWAR, the Navigation Warfare System."

Matt cranked his window down. A hot breeze blew through the car.

"What really opened everything up was in 1997 when the Russian company, Aviconversias, announced it could commercially distribute a jammer capable of blocking GPS signals within a radius of 200 kilometers. And that was back in '97. Imagine what they can do now.

"Another problem appeared, a sort of foreboding, when the military was testing some GPS stuff in the New York area. It caused a number of GPS receivers in civil aircraft to lose track of their signals while approaching Newark International Airport. And this jamming equipment was commercially available then. It isn't new, but all of a sudden there's this overwhelming interest in it.

"That stuff back then was primitive compared to the fine-tuning those wacko hackers can do now. Hell, they could slip just a few degrees off here and there, and who knows where the plane or ship would end up. Couple feet to the right or left at some of these airports and the crew and passengers on a foggy day or night could land on a restaurant instead of a runway."

Sunny looked at Matt and saw the passion and accompanying fear in his eyes for something he loved, the high-tech world of satellites and GPS signals and jammers out there that had to be caught.

"How nice for you to know all that good stuff, Matt. But I am still pissed and probably in some kind of post-traumatic thing, for all I know. Try to imagine how you would feel in my position. I'm hungry, damn it. At least you could feed me."

They ate part of their enormous sandwiches and watched the flow of traffic in and out of the deli. There was the sound of children, parents trying to control them and the smell of beer and coffee. Loud music played and made it difficult to hear. Two televisions, each on different stations, added to the noise pollution.

Waitresses looking bored and tired went through the motions of being cute and polite to those who wanted to flirt with them.

Matt and Sunny got up and walked over to a doorway that had a cardboard sign with the word "RESTROOMS" written on it in black magic marker. They walked down a dark flight of greasy linoleum stairs. "Just a couple of dirty little holes in the wall. Nowhere in this area to warehouse equipment for nefarious dithering purposes," Matt said. "Moisture on the walls, too, Sunny. I'd say we rule out the possibility of sensitive electronics surviving for very long down here. We'll look upstairs."

To the rear of the restaurant, just beyond a jukebox, was a purple door. A few other colors shone through where paint had been chipped off and layers were peeling. "That one might go to where we want to be," Matt said.

"You just going to ask if you can go upstairs and snoop?"

"How about we go stuff the jukebox, keep an eye on the people and then maybe one of us tries the door, see if it's locked? Better order a Coke or something. They took our sandwiches."

Sunny looked at Matt, lowered her head and raised her eyebrows. "And if it isn't? I mean, if it isn't open?"

"Well, we'll just see what happens."

A fat lady in a stain-streaked apron pressed a huge sandwich between her breasts to make it more bite-sized. She picked up a butcher knife, walked over to a table where a family of three was waiting. She put the sandwiches down on their table onto pieces of waxed paper and sliced each one down the middle. The kids laughed and clapped their hands.

Matt and Sunny left their drinks and the meager remains of their meal on the table and walked over to the jukebox. Matt put in some coins and randomly pushed buttons.

"You don't care what you play?" Sunny asked.

"Just put the money in and push buttons. We're not going to be here to listen to the tunes, anyhow. You coming up with me? You don't have to."

"I'm not quite ready to give up on you—yet," Sunny said.

The purple door was open. Matt and Sunny looked at the room of hungry customers before disappearing behind the door.

The big waitress noticed their table and the drinks. She scooped up some money Matt had left, dumped it in a kangaroo pouch on her apron and scanned the busy restaurant for them. She shrugged her shoulders and bundled some napkins into a big ball and headed for the garbage.

The stairway to Randolph's second-floor apartment was more multicolored than the entrance door. There was not only the layered paint, but also a multitude of wallpapers showing through. It smelled like cat urine.

A plastic curtain covered a window at the top of the stairs. Matt walked up to the door on the right and tapped it with a key. There was no answer. He hit it with his fist. On the third try he banged three times then took the class ring off his left hand.

"That hurts," he said.

"Maybe we should leave," Sunny said. "No, we stay. What am I thinking?"

Matt backed up to the dirty yellow railing. He put his hands behind his back, grabbed hold of the rail and kicked the door, just to the right of the doorknob. It made a cracking noise like a small caliber pistol when it broke at the lock point. It smacked the interior wall and stopped with a bang.

Matt and Sunny stood motionless, like there was a bump in the black night and if they remained quiet they would discover its origin and be able to protect themselves.

There was no protecting anything.

A man in yellow Bermuda shorts sat at a computer terminal facing the door. A yellow cat curled on top of the table beside him licking something white out of a cereal bowl. The man was barefoot and bare-chested with an aboriginal necklace around his neck. He wore a royal blue baseball cap that said

"Masterpiece Theater" in white letters. He held a big black pistol in his right hand and a glass of milk in his left. There was a thick odor of pot and bacon fat.

30

Matt felt his cell phone vibrate in his pocket. He figured it had to be Pat Shepherd.

Randolph kept the gun on Matt and Sunny. He sipped his milk, put it down beside the computer and reached over to stroke the cat.

"You don't look like burglars," he said. "You look like Saturday morning yuppies who don't really need to rob an apartment above a smelly deli. I'll bet you even have some money you haven't spent yet."

Matt looked around at the laptops, PCs, model aircraft and metal lathe. Empty frozen food boxes overflowed in corner wastebaskets and plastic shopping bags.

"We have the wrong room," Sunny said. "I thought you were someone else. My uncle—yes, my uncle, I think, lives here."

"Your uncle lives here? I'm the only one up here. Sorry, that just won't make it."

"Okay," Matt said. "You got us. Let's call the police. Here, we'll use my cell phone."

As Matt lowered his hand to the vibrating cell, Randolph leaned the gun toward Sunny.

"This gun is real quiet. Made the silencer myself. This is a .45 and the velocity of the ammo that comes out of here is subsonic. In other words, it does not produce a sonic 'crack.' That's what I like. Deadly and silent. So you see, the sound suppressor on the end of this baby does real good. I got the decibels and frequencies very finely tuned. This be my little whispering death right here, man.

"And you know what else? I'm real modern up here. I actually have a phone or two myself. We could use mine. But I don't think we'll need to do that. We can resolve this enigma in a more realistic manner, much less of a mess than involving the police—don't you think? Oh yes. If you don't get your hands back above your head I'll pull the trigger and you'll see just how good I am at making these little suppressors. Makes all the messy metal slivers worth it. Ever take a bite of metal on a filling in your mouth? Just wondered."

Randolph picked the cat up off his desk and threw it into a garbage-filled corner. The cat got up like it was used to it and started rummaging through the boxes. The flies didn't seem to bother the cat.

Matt put his hands back up.

"Yah know," Randolph said, "I'm confused. I really don't know what to do here. I shoot you two burglars dead and I'm probably okay. But if they find my homemade beauty here, there's a $10,000 fine and some jail time for the suppressor. Then I got all my computer stuff here. It's very close and very private to me. I know. Empty your pockets. Let me see who you are."

Sunny and Matt dutifully emptied their pockets. Randolph kept his gun on them and at the same time opened his window. Some light rain and hot air blew through. He lifted his arms.

"Always good to air out the pits once in awhile," he said. "Ben Franklin used to sit naked at open windows in storms. Air his ass and pits out real good."

Sunny and Matt took steps backward while Randolph rummaged through their belongings. He opened Sunny's wallet and dumped cards and money onto his desk.

"Oh, a pilot. I'll be damned. I have something to do with flying," he said.

He emptied the contents of Matt's wallet.

"You have to be shitting me," he said. "An ID for the Hughes Center? This is too much. A coincidence?"

He walked around to the other side of the desk.

"I think this is more than a simple burglary. Don't you? What are the odds? But no problem. I have a real good idea about how I can solve this. Young lady, you step over there in the corner, by the cat and the boxes. Turn around and put your hands on the wall. Mr. Hughes Center Guy, lay down on your stomach right there."

31

The door flew open and hit the crumbling plaster wall. Pat Shepherd stood in the middle of the doorway with his hands stuck deeply down into the pockets of his raincoat. He smiled and said, "Hello. Am I missing all the fun?"

"Come in," Randolph said. "I love company. This must be my lucky day. Who the hell are you?"

Shepherd walked slowly toward the opposite side of the room where the cat was picking and choosing what to eat out of the corner garbage.

"I'm with stupid, over there." Shepherd nodded his head toward the open door where a tall, blonde, middle-aged man stood holding a big gun, no silencer, pointed at Randolph.

Shepherd cleared his throat. "I have an announcement," he said. "The Pittsburgh Police and the state boys and girls will be here in a few minutes. Why don't we just put our stupid weapons down and wait? That way we won't shoot little holes in each other. Oh, and by the way, you might want to put that old .45 with the illegal silencer away, buddy. And how about some introductions?"

The television downstairs in the deli got louder. There were new smells of stale beer and meat, fresh frying grease.

"How about those introductions?" Shepherd said. "The new guy in the hall, the one with what I suspect is dyed-blonde hair, is the 'Wolfe' of the Week, a nickname he received in his college days. Retired FBI friend of mine. And, ah, I'll let the rest of you go ahead and introduce yourselves."

Matt glanced over to the corner where the cat was at a plastic tarp thrown over a six-foot object. "What's that?" he said to no one in particular.

"Nothing," the host of the party said. "Nothing. Just some art. Yeah, it has to do with art."

Wolfe walked over to the white sheet, grabbed it in the center and gave a tug. The sheet slid off and the object beneath it started to tip and fall toward him before the cover had completely fallen to the floor.

Wolfe pushed it up, balancing on both feet, straining his six-foot-four-inch frame. Once he got it upright, he slid the rest of the cover off and let it fall to the floor.

Everyone stood staring at it except Matt. He turned his head away and grabbed Sunny's hand and screamed. "My God! What is the matter with you? What in the name of all that is holy are you doing with that thing? There must be a law, something. It's just not right."

Randolph picked out a long strand of greasy hair obstructing the vision in his left eye. He placed it back on top of his head. "It's art. That's all, man, just art. You creeps just have no taste, no aesthetic soul. Perfectly legal, too."

"Legal—maybe," Shepherd said. "But you are a sick son of a bitch."

Wolfe turned his back to the exposed object and ran out of the room. There was the sound of choking and spitting in the hall. French fries and pickles.

Randolph looked at the remainder of people in the room. "Hey, the great Leonardo DaVinci was into this. What was good for Leonardo is good enough for me."

Matt joined Wolfe in the hall. There was the sound of steps ascending the stairs.

Sunny walked up to Randolph's desk and picked up her cell phone. Randolph put his .45 with the homemade silencer in his desk drawer.

"Hello," she said into the phone. "May I speak to Carl Farnley? Tell him Sunny Patronski is calling from Pittsburgh."

There was some mumbling and grumbling in the background and the scratching sound of a phone being slid over a desk.

"Hi, Sunny. Hear you're having a little difficulty there in Steeler Country."

"Carl, I thought of you just a minute or two ago. Had to call."

"What?" Farnley said.

"It's about this thing in the corner of a room I'm standing in. It's about what you live for, Carl. But it is something that will blow even your sick mind."

"Well isn't this cozy?" a voice said from the hallway. "Hope this crap in the hall here isn't evidence. Bag it and tag it? I don't think so."

A short fat man in a state police uniform stepped into the room pinching his nose in a mocking motion to avoid the unpleasant odor.

"Everyone seems to be getting along very well here. Let's just clean up the mess and have a party. Can I take my people and leave now? Why am I here?"

He looked into the corner at the sheet on the floor, then up at the object standing there, silent and still. He started to reach for his gun, then took his hand away, took out a red handkerchief and put it to his mouth.

"Oh my God," he said.

32

TV noise from downstairs in the deli went silent. Instead there was the sound of Elton John singing something about Jesus loves his money, so they say, and Levon blows up balloons all day.

Matt and Wolfe flashed some ID to a few straggling police coming up the stairs as they headed for the basement bathrooms. On their way down, they looked up at a muted flat-screened television attached to the wall just above the Coke machine.

There was a still photo of an attractive lady in an airline pilot uniform. She was standing in front of a Boeing 767. The split screen showed a family photo, obviously taken by a professional photographer, with an artificial background of a summer scene with waterfalls and the deep green leaves of midsummer. There were two children in the picture. One was a blonde wearing shorts with oversized cargo pockets. The husband held a little girl in his arms. Her hair was in pigtails. Everyone was smiling.

Sunny tucked her phone into her pocket. "Excuse me, officers. May I go powder my nose? This has been too much."

The fat state police officer with the red handkerchief motioned toward the door. "Fine," he said.

Sunny walked out into the deli to the noise and smells. The big waitress with the butcher knife looked at her and said, "What in the hell is going on up there? The weird doctor having a party or something?"

Sunny came through the single door leading to the second floor. She looked over at Matt and The Wolfe of the Week arguing with a man behind an old brass cash register. The man pointed at the jukebox and Matt pointed at the muted television.

"You're not in charge here, buddy," the cashier said. "Someone paid for that song and it's going to play. No television until I say so."

"I paid for the song," Matt said. "I put ten dollars in there so I have the right to out-volume the song I paid for. Get it?"

The cashier put both his hands on top of the bar and studied the rings on his fingers. He shook his head from left to right in a wide range of motion as he said, "You have a real problem here, don't you?"

"I sure do, buddy," Matt said. "Just turn the volume up."

"I'm not your buddy and you don't own this place and you don't own the volume or the copyright to the picture or the fucking French fries. Now, either you leave or I'll call the police. Better yet, I'll just walk upstairs and get some of the ones up there, unless it's another costume party going on. I mean, they are real cops, aren't they?"

Wolfe stood beside Matt pounding his fingers on the mahogany bar, waiting patiently.

"It's wired like that, buddy. Not that you need to know or that it's any of your goddamn business. When the box plays, the television mutes. If you want to hear the news, go into the next room, you lurpy bastard."

"Why didn't you tell me that in the first place?"

"You didn't ask me, sport," the cashier said.

It was almost one o'clock and the line in the deli entranceway was out the door and onto the street. A few families got up from their seats as Matt, Wolfe and Sunny brushed by them on a slow jog to the next room where, hopefully, the news was on—and un-muted.

Little children, families and a few teenagers sat quietly looking up, mesmerized at the black and white screen. The Lone Ranger sat on top of a big white horse rearing on its hind legs as the masked man repeated, "HI-HO-SILVER-AND-AWAY!"

Matt ran behind the bar, reached up to a ledge extending from the base of the television and picked up the flicker. He fingered channel two and a Budweiser commercial with frogs and lizards came on. He pushed Channel 4 and an aging, gray-haired anchorwoman with large black earrings looked down at her news copy with a tragic look on her face.

The cashier from the brass cash register turned the corner and headed toward Matt. Two small children in the back of the room cried and pointed to the television and said something about The Lone Ranger.

The cashier grabbed the flicker from Matt's hands as the lady with the earrings on Channel 4 said with a throaty quiver in her voice, as though she could break into tears at any minute, "Captain Lorraine Harding is survived by her husband and two children. A memorial service will be held..."

Matt shoved the cashier out of the way as he, Wolfe and Sunny ran toward the front door. When they cleared the waiting crowd, Sunny stopped and grabbed both Wolfe and Matt by their arms.

"Wait," she said. "Where are we going? What are we doing?"

All three looked at each other. Matt said, "Back to the Hughes Center in Cape May. No. I don't know. We have the man here in his apartment. Did you see that stuff? He's the one. I'm telling you. He has to be. This is where it all triangulates and with the stuff in that apartment, I know he is."

Sunny moved her hand up onto Matt's shoulder. Matt looked at it for a long moment.

"Matt, I'm still here. I'm not going anywhere without you."

Wolfe patted them both on their shoulders. "Well, I'm the new guy and you two don't even know me or what I'm doing here. But let me tell you. Unless you want to be arrested for burglary, we'd better keep moving because you broke into that asshole's apartment, and if what Shepherd told me is correct, there isn't going to be anything there that the state boys are going to find suspicious—just a weirdo with lots of computers, GPS stuff and...oh, yes, that monster in the corner."

They walked down Midland Street on a narrow sidewalk paralleling the Banana Warehouse, passed the Spaghetti Bar and turned right onto Steel Park Place. They got into Wolfe's rental.

"Where we going?" Wolfe said.

"I have to talk to Farnley," Sunny said. "He'll know about Dr. Bertrum Randolph's hobby. I don't really want to ask but there may be a link. I can't imagine what, but there must be. Who could even sleep in that place with that thing in the corner?"

"And the captain on Channel 4," Matt said. "Her family. The kids, those beautiful kids. For what? And the creep that did the dithering has to be upstairs. Has to be."

"Correct, my friend," Wolfe said. "But you're not going to prove anything behind bars. And something else, you know you really do lose credibility when you are arrested for burglary and pull some of the stunts you did at the deli. Why don't you let me and Shepherd handle the whole thing? We're used to it."

"Listen, Wolfe," Matt said. "I don't even know exactly who you are yet, and I know you're risking a lot, and I don't know why that is, either. But I haven't been accused of anything and those police didn't read our rights and they didn't say halt or stop in the name of whatever. If I was being arrested, it's news to me. Anyhow, come along for the ride. This is *my* problem and it is *my* suspicion, very strong suspicion, that that beautiful lady with the family is dead because of something I'm associated with back in Atlantic City. And I am going to take care of it if it kills me."

"Poor choice of words," the Wolfe of the Week said. "You don't want to end up like the artwork in the corner, the way it just stands there, dead like some plastic monster, just there for someone's enjoyment. Sick isn't the word to use here. You think something like cannibalism is distasteful? No pun intended. Hell, those cannibals at least ate it. They didn't sit it around to watch it all day. They were candy-asses compared to the whackos that are into this crap."

33

It wasn't hard for Sunny to steal a plane that belonged to her in the first place. It was parked outside the state police hangar, in the yellow slot, exactly where the obsessive-compulsive custodian told her to tie it down.

The large hangar doors were closed but a man-door a few feet from her Cirrus stood open. There was the hum of a window air conditioner coming from the back of the hangar where some officers sat drinking coffee in the small office.

Sunny crawled into the plane first, then Matt and finally Wolfe went to the rear and strapped in. There was no flight plan, only a clearance from the tower and a few minutes with Pittsburgh Approach while Sunny navigated through the Pittsburgh controlled airspace.

The flight to Cape May was low and slow to keep out of radar. She knew there probably wasn't a need to hide from anyone, but according to movies she saw, it just seemed like the thing to do.

"Nothing illegal about low and slow as long as we're not too low and slow," she said to her passengers as they watched scenery pass below.

"Why so low?" Wolfe asked. "It's bumpy at this altitude in these mountains. I mean, it's your airplane. Isn't it? I hope."

"Yeah, it's mine. My grandfather left it to me."

"Good."

At the low altitude all three passengers were hot, even with the door missing, the result of the crowbar break-in. Sunny's trick of leaving the door unlocked didn't work.

The noise was loud and some charts and candy wrappers blew through the cockpit. Wolfe took a few swipes at the flying objects.

Sunny flipped up the right cup of her headpiece as she dialed Farnley's number with her thumb.

"Who's flying the plane?" Wolfe said into his mike.

"Autopilot—not to worry," Sunny said.

Medical Examiner Farnley picked up the phone in Cape May.

"Sunny here, neighbor," she said over the sound of wind blowing into the aircraft.

She explained what she thought she saw in Dr. Bertrum Randolph's apartment. She left out details about the GPS, laptops and other tech equipment above the deli and concentrated on those things she knew Farnley would find so much more tantalizing—and potentially useful.

"You've seen your first true work of plastinated art, Sunny girl. Sometimes this new field of art makes viewers cold stone pass out. Some exhibitors have told me they hit the deck at the rate of one a day. That makes a real statement, doesn't it? Talk about powerful art."

"Meet me at the airport, Cape May, Carl. I know this is nothing to you, but it is extremely upsetting to me and we're thinking it may have a link to one airline disaster today at Pittsburgh and potentially many more to come. We're not sure of the connection. Anyhow, meet me and don't bring anyone with you. And, oh yes, Carl, none of us here are going to be in the mood to eat and we're especially not going to be in the mood to watch you stuff your face. Love you, neighbor. See you there."

"Sunny, wait," Carl said. "Don't hang up yet. Please tell me this is true. Did you get any pictures of it? Did it have any jewelry around the neck or on the fingers? Anything in the genital area stand out?"

"Just meet us, Carl. There will be me, Matt, and Special Agent Wolfe. Actually, retired Agent Wolfe. I'll explain."

Turbulence picked up the lower they got on the east side of the mountains. As they approached the Washington, D.C., area, Sunny opened the throttle to increase her speed. She took special attention to take a detour around the controlled airspace in the restricted areas she followed on the charts and electronic indicators. She divided her attention between the flickering navigation screens and the tops of the trees and power lines beneath her. They were looking closer than she liked.

"Plastination?" Matt said. "What's that mean? And what is the point of a full size corpse in a giant jar?"

34

At a Catholic church ten blocks from Randolph's deli apartment, a Requiem Mass was being held as Sunny, Wolfe, and Matt skirted the presidential airspace on their way to Cape May County Airport.

The mass was held in evangelical protest of the plasticized bodies that were to be displayed at a warehouse in the Strip District of Pittsburgh.

Ezekiel Framland, curator of the collection that had been displayed in Germany, Austria, Spain and Switzerland, was to arrive in Pittsburgh in anticipation of the event.

No one attending the mass knew about the body that was proudly displayed above the restaurant. They were also unaware of the extent of the shipment of plastinated art about to arrive in Pittsburgh. Their expectation was maybe two or three, but fifty bodies encapsulated in hermetically-sealed, plastic containers would have made the mass potentially turn into a religious demonstration with violent potential.

In the back of the church, mumbling under his breath in Polish, an old man with a long gray handlebar mustache folded his hands in pious repose. He cleared his throat and unwrapped a cough drop, put it in his mouth and threw the wrapper on the floor. He blew his nose and cursed in Polish about his cold, the sniffling and goddamn sneezing.

The small girl sitting on his right looked up at him and shook her head.

"Bad man," she said. "Litterbug."

"Honey," the mother of the little girl whispered. "That's none of your business. Now you apologize to the nice old man."

He reached over and patted the girl's head and tugged at her ponytail.

"That's okay, darlin'. Y'all have a right. Litterbug? Huh. Sweet little thing, you are. Here, little one. Have a cough drop."

The priest said something about millions of people in Germany going to see the bodies displayed as art. A boy stood beside the priest and handed him a silver cone containing incense. The priest took the chain and blessed his congregation.

The old man with the cold walked to the back of the church, dipped both of his hands into the holy water, washed his hands over his face and slicked his hair back with the remaining moisture. He took his cowboy hat off a coat rack in the church foyer.

"Those fucking plastination nuts deserve to die," he mumbled as he walked down the steps into the bright sunlight of a clear and hot Pittsburgh day. "Then again, the money isn't bad."

He headed for the deli section of the Strip, coughing and blowing his nose. When he turned the corner, he expected to see a line of church people waiting to take their families to lunch. Instead there were protesters waiting to see the plastinated bodies they despised.

The old man with the hat stood, stroked his long mustache and watched.

There was a white van with Roman numerals and phone numbers stenciled on the doors and hood. Two satellite dishes extended from the roof. A short, blonde, attractive, heavily made-up woman stood in front of the van. She had a microphone in her hand. She shoved it into the face of a demonstrator holding a sign that read: "PLASTINATION ART—WORK OF THE DEVIL."

"We are concerned about the dignity of the dead," the man said.

"But, sir," the reporter said, "I understand these bodies were donated by volunteers, naturally before they died, and they knew exactly what they were doing. Don't they have a right? This is America."

A child standing by the man cried. He turned away from the reporter and took the child into his arms. She was crying hysterically. The father stroked some strands of hair out of her face and kissed her forehead.

"Did your news station take any photos of the 'anatomically precise' fetus displayed in the last Denver exhibit?" he said. "Or, how about the plastinated woman sitting at a table eating pizza? You taking your children to see that one?"

The girl cried louder and struck her father on the chest. He turned away from the reporter and walked into the crowd holding the little girl tightly in his arms.

Trog Svalden blew his nose on the street, looked around at the demonstrators, the Pittsburgh police and the media. He stepped into a phone both at the entrance of the Fish And Fry Warehouse, tore his mustache off and put it in his hip pocket. He sneezed. Out of his Flight-Deck red flack jacket he took a CD ROM, snapped it out of the case and stroked it as though it were a helpless puppy. Printed neatly with black ink on a simple envelope address sticker was: "Randolph Productions."

Wonder what flight is bringing the miserable fucking sinner exhibit into town? he thought. *Supply-side economics.*

35

Sunny and her passengers approached Cape May County Airport. She looked down and turned to her runway heading. Farnley's car was in the parking lot. He was leaning on the hood, fanning his face with something.

Sunny taxied over to the ramp and headed to where she had seen Farnley leaning on the car. He wasn't there. He was under a maple tree in the center of the lot, braced on the trunk with his shirt unbuttoned to his navel. There was a gold Orthodox cross around his wet neck. He motioned to them to come to him under the tree.

They walked over to the maple, happy to feel some wind hitting their faces as they sat down beside Farnley. He looked at Sunny, said his hellos and extended his hand to Matt. He looked up at Wolfe.

"Carl, this is retired Special Agent Wolfey. He's the Wolfe of the Week to his friends and retired co-workers. He's a friend of Pat's—Pat Shepherd."

Carl Farnley remained seated and extended his hand to Wolfe. "Sit down, folks," he said. "I'm not going anywhere. There's a nice breeze. We can talk here as well as anywhere else."

Matt, Wolfe and Sunny made a semicircle in front of Farnley. Farnley took a deep breath and said, "So you want to hear about plastination, do you?"

"Well, Carl, it is not that we really want to," Sunny said. "There is more that we think is related to it, but we're still looking."

Farnley shifted his stomach from left to right. "Now, I want everyone to understand that I am not trying to offend. I'm going to tell it like it is and not many people know this stuff. It's no big secret, but we just don't hear it or maybe we just don't want to hear it."

Carl took out his handkerchief and dabbed his face and chest. He tried to pull his pants up over his hanging gut. "Art is in the eye of the beholder," he said. "A Professor Vandervolden, I don't know from what university, started this thing where people volunteer their bodies so they can be displayed as art after they die. He preserves them by skinning them, and then splays the inside of the corpse. Sometimes all the corpse isn't displayed. Sometimes, just parts. Some are actually arranged in life situations where they're eating pizza, shaving in the morning—that sort of thing. I read somewhere that he has some even more interesting positions in exclusive showings."

Wolfe maneuvered on the grass, tried to get comfortable and said, "Parts is parts."

No one laughed.

"Kinda like recycling, some people think," Farnley said. "Sort of like transcendental. You know, the wind blows, the earth gets wet, evaporates, becomes a cloud, it rains, someone dies and is planted and the entire cycle starts all over again. In other words, there is no death."

Matt, Sunny and Wolfe simultaneously turned toward each other. They said nothing and looked back at Carl.

Carl patted his wet head to keep the salty perspiration from flowing down and stinging his eyes. "Anyone have any gum?" he asked.

Sunny slapped him on the knee. "Go on, Carl. Gum and food later."

"This is getting bigger and bigger," Carl said. "This guy has had his work all over the world. Japan, Russia, Belgium. All over the place. Actually the way it works, the preservation, is very simple. Any high school biology class could do the same thing.

"The subject is soaked in formaldehyde, frozen, thawed out and then dissected. Works like a charm. Of course, they have to remove the fat and water from the specimen and replace it with plastic, thus the term 'plastination.' What is left is an odorless, semi-erect specimen that's flexible enough to be formed into an artistic piece and then let to stand alone. You should see it. It is one amazing sight."

"Carl," Matt said. "We did see one in an apartment in the Strip District in Pittsburgh while we were working on what was, up until a few hours ago, a potential aviation accident."

Sunny stood up and brushed some grass off her slacks. "Potential is not the correct word any longer," she said. "The accident, we don't think, was in fact an accident, and we have reason to believe the guy with the stiff, or semi-stiff, in the corner was in on it."

"Airplanes and corpses," Carl said. "Not too far separated."

Sunny did a few calisthenics on the grass, trying to limber up, unwind, relax, de-plastinate. She told Carl about the safety of flying compared to having sex when you're overweight. The men watched Sunny. They didn't talk until she stopped bending and stretching.

"Very funny, Sunny," Carl said. He leaned on his elbow and his stomach sagged to the ground. He didn't seem to mind. Some blades of grass stuck to him.

"Listen," he said. "Not everyone is as sensitive about death as we are. I saw on the BBC where some town in Europe, I think it was Pakrovsk—a guy died in a hostel and they let him sit at the kitchen table for seven days because they couldn't get anyone to come for the body. The dead guy sat in front of a cereal bowl for a week, for God's sake. Imagine that."

"Yeah," Wolfe said. "Now, moving right along."

Carl continued, undiscouraged. "No one would come for the guy because he was homeless. The police said they weren't equipped for that sort of thing, wasn't their job. Public utilities said they didn't deal with homeless corpses. So the poor guy was there in front of the cereal bowl until someone called the militia and they took the thing out of there. God bless America."

The wind blew hard as Matt, Wolfe and Sunny stood up and brushed themselves off.

Sunny looked at Matt. "You haven't said much of anything."

"I don't feel good," he said and headed for the Rent-A-Wreck sign.

"Hey, listen," Carl said. "In the same report I saw where this guy had an accident and lost a lot of his penis. He sacrificed his index finger to have it transplanted. The finger—in place of."

"Carl," Sunny said. "If you don't stop I am going to ask this trained FBI guy to beat the crap out of you."

Carl raised his eyebrows and pretended he was zippering his lips closed. Sunny bent over and kissed his wet forehead.

"See you around, big boy," she said. "Maybe you can tell us about anthrax and mutant spores next time we have a fun afternoon under a maple tree."

"Oh, man, Sunny. Listen to this one."

Sunny and Wolfe turned and walked quickly to catch up to Matt. Sunny stuck her fingers in her ears. Hear no evil.

36

The Sloshingburger wasn't crowded for lunch when they walked in. Everyone was baking on the beach, planning on their painful burns turning into glorious golden skin.

The large canvas awning covering the Sloshingburger slapped and whipped in the steady ocean winds. The waiters and waitresses scurried around placing bricks covered in colorful fabric onto menus and napkins that would otherwise blow away.

Two waiters, dressed in T-shirts that were silk-screened to look like tuxedos, untied a rope and let thick plastic windows unroll to the ground. One of the waiters came over to Sunny and knelt down beside her as though it was easier to communicate in such a position.

He spoke with a German accent, was about twenty years old, blonde and muscular. He could have modeled for a weightlifting magazine, the front cover.

"Hey, and how you guys doing?" he said. "What a beach day. Appetizers, drinks all around?"

Wolfe got up, walked around to where the energetic waiter knelt and got on his knees beside the young man.

"Why do you people kneel like this? I see it in Georgetown, too. Is it a religious thing, or what?"

The waiter laughed a sincere laugh and stood up. He looked down into Wolfe's dark eyes.

"No, sir. They tell us to do it. They said the customers feel closer to you when you do and they tell us we'll get more tips that way. I'm finishing up my undergraduate degree in electrical engineering in Hamburg. Come here every summer to work. I'll do just about anything for a good tip. Kneeling is no big deal. I'll sit on the floor if you want me to."

Matt made a wide sweeping motion with his hand, a priest gesturing to the flock. "You may stand and be counted, young man," he said. "You will be rewarded either prone, prostrate or erect."

"Poor choice of words," Wolfe said. "Upright, or better yet vertical, might sound less anatomical."

Everyone laughed. Wolfe dusted off his knees and sat down.

"Three Sloshingburgers and an order of thin onion rings as an appetizer," Sunny said. "Anyone want a beer or something?"

Wolfe ordered a Guinness and Matt a Michelob Ultra. Sunny ordered lemonade.

"Here's the thing," Wolfe said. "I got in on this for an old friend, your friend, Pat. We've been through a lot together. We did the OSI, you know, The Office of Special Investigation in the Air Force, and we both went into the agency together. He liked guns and I liked intelligence.

"Intelligence became hours and days and months of stakeouts, probably the most bore-ass time of my life. The incessant boredom was, however, punctuated with brief moments of intense fear and panic.

"Anyhow, we need to get on this thing and quit pissing around. Either we're in a game of catch the dithering wacko who is wrecking airliners and has the potential to reroute, if I understand correctly, military warheads.

"Now, you know none of this is rocket science. Matt, you are the brain but also the man with no plan. Sunny, Matt, both of you—I'm picking up these vibes, like these elemental things about affection, anger, getting even, holding hands, not holding hands. I need you two to make up your minds and quit the teenage games here. I can't do this with Romeo and Juliet at the beach. Make up or don't. Stick with it. Make a commitment to this job and to each other and let's move on, or I am history. Got it?"

Sunny sprinkled Parmesan cheese on her plate, shook some ketchup over it and stirred it all together with a fork. She dabbed an onion ring into the mess and took a large bite. She sipped her lemonade.

The handsome waiter brought two beers in frosted mugs. He put them down as though he was proud to serve the brew. He said to Matt, "*Zu Ihrer Gesundheit. Getrank wie Fische*."

"What?" Matt said. "I took Spanish. Don't have a clue as to what you said."

"To your health. Drink like fish," the waiter said.

As soon as the German waiter left, Wolfe sipped his beer. He looked at Matt and Sunny after dabbing the foam off his upper lip.

"First of the day," he said. "Listen, you two are really something. You must have grown up in this world where you believe everything you hear. You and your parents had their lily-white asses, all perfect and puckered and dimpled. The sun shone on the beach and there were no flies and very few lies, let alone crimes to deal with. Maybe someone snatched your surfboard or whatever the hell you call it. But, that's about it. The rest of the time it was probably Dick and Jane at the fucking seashore."

Sunny squeezed extra lemon into her third lemonade.

"I have to pee," she said. Her voice was sing-song and gave an I-don't-give-a-shit impression. "Are you upset with us because we aren't worldly, Wolfe? We can't all be named Wolfe, be a retired federal agent, and be intuitively suspicious and negative. How have you formed all these opinions about us? We've only met you a half day ago."

Sunny didn't wait for an answer. She slid her chair back and headed for the ladies' room. "And oh, Wolfey," she said, "My ass gets tanned in the summer, nice and brown, all over, too. Maybe a dimple there. Ask Matt. I don't know if he'll get another look at it again, though. I go to the roof of my condo. No panty line. All natural. Think you're a smart-ass?"

Wolfe and Matt laughed and watched Sunny strut to the washroom. She took long, exaggerated strides and turned her head to look at them while she strolled. She smiled a big, white-teeth smile. When she came back, Matt was drawing vectors and satellites and a compass rose on a Sloshingburger napkin.

"Okay, here it is," Wolfe said. "The fat guy. What's his name? Fartley? I'm sorry—Farnley. That's it. You said he had some kind of bullshit story about the corpse smelling like turpentine or paint. You said something about him never painting around the condo. You said he conned you into this flight to Pittsburgh where a plastination art show is going on at the same time you get a body stolen. And what did he just tell us about part of the plastination process—the chemicals used to preserve? Or maybe he's saying the corpse had paint on it that he didn't completely remove. Like really, come again? He didn't want to rub too hard, didn't want to hurt the sensitive turf of the stiff. And by the way, what the hell is a guy on his way to a fishing tournament, the Clayton Meadows guy, what's he doing going fishing covered in so much paint that when he dies, you can smell it through a crime scene bag? And Sunny, I'm sorry about what I said about your ass. It is very nice and I'm sure it is brown in the summer. I am sorry. I was out of order. I'm retired, aging. Cut me some slack."

Sunny reached over the table and put her hand on the Wolfe's forearm. She looked at how long and blonde the hair was. *Wolfe Man hair,* she thought, and patted him gently.

"Let's go to my condo for some wine. You're right about the plan. We have to talk."

"What plan?" Matt asked.

37

The yellow plastic police line that surrounded Randolph's deli apartment and the restaurant was down. People stepped over it. Some tore off pieces; shoved them into their pockets.

An old man in a Unified Gas Company jacket carrying a red toolbox walked up to the butcher-knife waitress.

"Ma'am, it's Unified here. Possible gas thing going on upstairs." He had a slight southern drawl. "That nasty flex furnace up there be pretty old. Probably just a pressure fitting come loose, lady. Some plumbers' putty do the job." He walked toward the door leading to Randolph's apartment.

The waitress started to walk after him, then saw the cook motioning to two large pieces of roast beef and a bowl of coleslaw.

"It's ready," the cook said.

She reached into her apron for the knife.

"Where's my knife?" she said to the cook. "You playing with me again, Ralphie?"

When the plumber walked into Dr. Randolph's room, it was obvious the place had been searched. Randolph was in the corner anchoring a piece of plastic over the top of the plasticized corpse. The cat was doing some general, explorative sniffing. Its tail was high in the air. It was nibbling something red and meaty off the floor. The smell of urine, French fries and formaldehyde filled Trog Svladen's nostrils.

"Now who the hell are you?" Bertrum Randolph said. "Is this another stupid parade or what? I guess it is piss-poor taste in uniform day, isn't it?"

He walked over to Svladen and stuck his head down real close to the nametag on the gray shirt.

Svladen bent down and put his red toolbox on the floor. He reached into his pocket and carefully removed a butcher knife.

Randolph jumped back.

"What the fuck kind of plumbing tool is that, for Christ's sake?"

"What would you know about Christ?" Svladen asked quietly into Randolph's ear as he stuck only the tip of the blade into the lower abdomen. "As a matter of fact, either I get the other CD or you get some more butcher knife holes in you."

"Don't," Dr. Randolph said. "I can't handle pain."

"Don't even wimper," he said. "That's barely a scratch. We can do a lot better than that. Matter of fact, either I get the rest of the CDs with the GPS programs on them or you're going to start leaking a lot of blood."

Dr. Randolph put his left hand over his paisley T-shirt. He watched the blood drip to the floor where the cat patiently waited.

He started to scream, "You cut..."

38

Shepherd stood on the steps leading to the deck of Sunny's condo on Beach Drive. He poked numbers into his cell phone. He looked up and saw Sunny turn the corner.

"Oh, there you are," he said. "Was just going to call and let you know I was here. Figured you'd show up eventually."

Sunny slapped Shepherd on the back and stepped over a laptop sitting beside him. She unlocked the front door, and turned around to the men standing over her like they were waiting in line at a grocery store. "I'll get us some drinks. Let's sit out here and come up with this plan that Wolfe Man thinks we need so desperately."

She pushed the play button on the answering machine. There were four messages. The last one was Farnley mumbling something about information he should have told them when they were under the maple tree.

"Sunny," the message said, "one more thing. Body snatchers. Bodies are being stolen these days. Like at some big universities people are getting in trouble. They have these 'willed body' programs and people will their bodies to science. Well see, some unscrupulous bastards are doing what you could call 'grand theft dead body' and they're making big money on it. There's this guy in California who sold five hundred bodies, or parts of bodies. Made some money, I'd say. Military uses them to test land mines and some auto testers use them…"

Sunny pushed the "skip" button on her machine. Maybe someone else could listen later.

She put the iced teas on a tray and carried them to the deck. The three men were sprawled out on lounge furniture, sure to shade themselves with the umbrella buffeting in the ocean breeze.

"Everyone comfortable?" she asked. "Don't mind me. I'll just burn in the sun. You guys just make sure you're all cozy in the shade. I don't mind sitting in the sun. I can sweat as well as the next guy."

Wolfe and Shepherd nudged Matt. He kept toying with Shepherd's laptop. Shepherd slapped him hard on the back.

"Get up. Your girlfriend, well kinda girlfriend, is hinting."

"Please," Matt said. "Sit here, Sunny. Please."

Sunny placed the tray on a plastic coffee table. "There was a message from Carl," she said. "Said he forgot some details about our maple tree meeting at the airport. You don't want to hear about it. I take that back. You do want to hear about it. I don't. Body snatchers. Body thieves in the night—unreal."

Matt closed the laptop and slapped his hands together.

"I've been thinking. I don't care who looks guilty, who has a morbid interest in bodies, who is dating, not dating, angry, ambivalent about relationships. Wolfe is right. I can only care about one thing at this point and one thing only."

Everyone on the deck heard Shepherd crunching his ice cubes. While he crunched, he held one on the back of his neck. The moisture dripped down onto the front and back of his shirt and tie.

Matt continued. "I want to get the tapes or CDs or hard drives that have the codes for the GPS interfaces. That's all. There doesn't have to be anything else. We know it is either around the Atlantic City area or Pittsburgh, and as far as we know, there is one son of a bitch planning on selling the information, or themselves and their skills, to the highest bidder. At least we hope there's only one."

Shepherd spit some ice back into his glass and watched it sit there. "The stuff is probably on a CD," he said. "Couldn't get much information on a disk. And why would they put it on a hard drive and carry a CPU around trying to hide it from the authorities?"

"Don't need to take the CPU," Matt said. "Just the memory. But where is this going? We just have to find who is doing it and stop them. So what if it's on a tape, CD or memory? Who gives a rat's ass? What's it matter? We're not trying to pass a test here. We're trying to prevent the indiscriminate deaths of innocent people."

"Maybe not so indiscriminate," Wolfe said. "If these people are not terrorists, if they are just economically motivated, there will be blackmail. That's one thing. But if they want to influence the course of history, they can do it if they use their brains and keep their mouths shut after each incident."

"Incident?" Sunny said.

“Yeah, incident,” Wolfe said. “There might not be anything for six months or a year. Maybe longer. Then it is in their best interest to take down a plane, splash an ocean liner, depending on who or what is onboard. Hell, Air Force One isn’t even immune to this. They may have inertial navigation and all sorts of backup and crosschecks. But this dithering system is in its infancy compared to where it’s going to potentially end up one of these days. Actually, we’re only stalling for time, when you think about it. Eventually we’re, I mean the government, is going to come up with excellent scrambling stuff to keep the GPS hackers out of commercial and military hair. But until then, we have a real problem.”

"I hate to bring it up,” Sunny said, “but where are these damn bodies and plastination artists or whatever you call it coming from? What do they have to do with anything?”

“I don’t like Farnley,” Wolfe said. “There is something there I do not like.”

Sunny bit into a piece of lemon and puckered her lips.

“Wolfe,” she said. “He is weird. But this guy doesn’t know a byte from a bite or a GPS from a bowl of noodle soup. He’s a good man and one of many of your breed who isn’t a sports fan; likes morbid history instead. Doesn’t make him all bad, does it? Well, he’s into other stuff, other sports. Besides, we’re not here to talk about personalities. We need to talk about facts, just facts.”

“Out of the box,” Matt said. “We have to think out of the box about this. Here’s what we have: bodies, Randolph in the Strip, missing memory or CDs or tapes. We have nothing else but plastination art.”

“Don’t forget the fugue,” Matt said. “Don’t forget, no pun intended, Dr. Dowler. Poor Clark shows up in a bed-and-breakfast inn in Newport with a case of Budweiser and cheap cigars. He doesn’t smoke. Doesn’t know who he is and has jobs highlighted in the local paper. Guy has a PhD and highlights pizza delivery, farm hand, and dental assistant. All coincidence?”

“The bodies,” Sunny said. “Or, I mean, the body at Randolph’s place on the Strip? If you were a mad professor type, where would you hide a disk or CD?”

Matt looked at her. “You mean maybe it is placed in the body?” He raised an eyebrow. “I guess it could be placed—anywhere—in the body.”

39

Matt pulled the Rent-A-Wreck into his parking spot at the Hughes Center on Monday morning. Shepherd pulled in beside Dr. Wilhamena Halstead, who was putting the convertible top up on her Miata. When she saw Matt and Shepherd, she stretched further than she needed to and bent down to pick up nothing on the ground, her tight skirt lifting upward.

Matt looked over at Shepherd and mouthed, "Welcome home, big boy. Her Repugnance has arrived."

Matt noticed his name had been removed from the small sign in front of his slot.

Dr. Halstead walked over to the Rent-A-Wreck before Matt had time to get out. She pressed her stomach against his door, folded her arms, leaned them on the open sunroof and looked down at Matt through the hole in the roof.

"Matt, you're here to visit? How nice for us. Or, maybe, get your stuff? We have it in a corner of your office in boxes. I can have Jeff help you carry it to your car if you want."

Matt didn't know whether to look at her stomach sticking part-way into the car or look up at her face.

"Dr. Halstead, I was upset the other day."

He looked up at her face then down at her stomach. She shifted her weight and her stomach situated closer to him.

"I know I've been kinda stupid. I am sorry, ma'am. And you know that 767 freighter that went down at PIT and I'm really on that."

Dr. Halstead pressed harder against the door of the Rent-A-Wreck. "Well, that is all well and good, Matt. And you do excellent work. No question about that. However, you are not security, CIA, FBI, ATF or anything else but a technician, and a good one. You are top notch. But, my dear, you aren't a part of the investigative branch of anyone's government, especially ours."

Halstead knelt down and stuck her face into the car. "And you do not have the authority to charter, lease or accommodate your flying needs in an expensive jet to tote you all over the countryside because you need a ride. The Citation is expensive, Matt. We use it sparingly. You have overstepped some boundaries here in more than one area. And I don't appreciate calls from police about my people. These calls from Pittsburgh make me uncomfortable. You know how I feel about you, Matt. By the way, how is that girlfriend of yours—ah, Silly, Sherry—what is it?"

"Sunny," Matt said. "But I think she's pissed at me, too."

"Just not your day with the ladies, is it big guy," Wilhamena said.

Shepherd walked up to the car and extended his hand to Wilhamena. "Looks like the prodigal son has returned, boss. That is great. Hope he is back to stay."

"The prodigal is trying to return, Shepherd. He's trying but I'm not sure I can afford him. He lies to accommodate himself when it comes to chartering jets and therefore botches up my flight budget, and he seems to have become a private eye or Fed investigator wannabe. When your employees start costing you money instead of making it, something has to be done. And when they start giving themselves assignments that *I* haven't assigned them, they have overstepped, and may just be out of the game."

Dr. Halstead turned back to Matt and bent down to look him in the eyes again. "Unless, of course, there is a reason to keep them around."

"Dr. Halstead," Matt said. "I have another problem, too. I was thinking about the dithering and the potential consequences of codes and knowledge getting into the wrong hands. Then I thought about how that was just the beginning. I thought about what would happen if the wrong people find out we're also working on the scrambling sequence at the Center and not just the Wide and Local Area Augmentation Systems. All our eggs are in one basket, for God's sake. They get to the building or to the research, and we're done. We haven't even thought of a backup."

"Here we go again," Wilhamena said.

Shepherd looked into the back seat of the car and said, "What smells in here? What stinks in that car, Matt?"

"It's a rental, Shep, just a rental. God only knows what smells back there. I didn't do anything." He started to open the door of the car.

Matt and Shepherd exchanged glances. Shepherd shook his head and said into Matt's ear as Wilhamena reached into her purse for a cigarette, "Just distracting Her Regurgitence, the Boss. But what the hell does smell, Matt? Something in the trunk?"

40

Sunny and the retired Wolfe propped their feet up on Sunny's front deck, watching morning beach joggers and kite flyers. There was the occasional early umbrella person staking out their beach claim for the day, reserving a few square feet of heaven. They'd shove the umbrella pole into the sand, wiggle it deeply, open up folding chairs and leave for coffee at the Aquatic Hot Dog across the street.

Wolfe tilted his coffee mug back and sipped the last little bit from the bottom. "Can I get you a cinnamon roll, a croissant or something at the Hot Dog Shop, Sunny?"

He grabbed a roll of hairy fat on his abdomen and said, "I want you to know this isn't all fat. There is something else in there, some harder fat and even lower, a little bit of muscle layered in there that's left over from the old weight-lifting days."

"Thanks for sharing that, Wolfe. I'll keep it in mind if I ever need a balding, blonde, hairy, tall man with some hard layered fat and muscle."

"Never know when it will come in handy," Wolfe said. "I'll walk over and get us some rolls."

Wolfe stood up and stretched, sucked his belly in and yawned. He slipped his on wingtips that didn't quite match his swimming suit and hairy chest. He walked over and patted Sunny on the shoulder.

"It's all I brought for the beach as far as shoes go," he said. "I'll pick up some matching pink flamingo shorts and muscle shirt later."

"Please, just the cinnamon rolls," Sunny said.

Wolfe disappeared around the corner of the condo, his shoelaces dragging behind the cordovan wingtips. Just as he turned the corner, a man with a red handlebar mustache and shaved head with orange freckles sprinkled on top appeared on the sidewalk. He had a small notebook in his hand. He looked at the notebook, then at the condos, then back at the notebook. He shook his head and rubbed his perspiring baldness. He started to walk away but stopped when he saw Sunny with her feet propped up on the railing.

"Oh, missy, can you help me?" he said. "Seems I just might be at the wrong address here. Lookin' to buy me a car and this here place, I don't know, it just doesn't fit the bill. That Beach Drive out there?"

"Sure," Sunny said. "Who you looking for? I have to get my sunglasses. Have a seat out here. Be right with you."

"No problem, little missy," the man said. "Take your good old time. Not that anxious to spend my money."

The cell phone snapped onto Sunny's shorts vibrated as she reached for her sunglasses. She put on her glasses and answered the phone.

"Sunny, Matt here. I'm walking to my office where my stuff, according to the boss, is packed in boxes nicely, just for my convenience."

"Doesn't sound like you've been very successful so far. Maybe turn on the charm," she said.

"Never say die," Matt said.

Sunny felt the hand brush her shoulder on its way to her cell phone.

"Sunny, you there? I have four bars here. Reception is excellent. Hello? Damn phone."

"Excuse me, mister. I don't think I invited you in."

"No problem, little lady. No problem at all. I just went ahead and let myself in."

The stranger put the phone in his hip pocket, walked over to the French doors leading to Sunny's front deck, closed them and flipped the deadbolt to the lock position.

"There now, sit. We'll talk," he said to Sunny as she walked around the corner with the large knife in her left hand.

"Now look what you've done. You've gone and taken a knife to a gun and electronic zapper fight. So, either put it down or I'll zap you and if you fight it, I'll shoot you, but not mortally wound you. So, I must say, it might hurt and very possibly could leave a scar. And I must say, I have seen your beautiful body in the all together, and you shouldn't scar that flesh. All I need is some information from you and your boyfriend, and maybe a CD or two."

Sunny slammed the knife down on the kitchen table. "You're the weirdo who had me in that motel room."

"Correctamundo, my fine lady. I must admit I was the man in the chair beside you."

"What do you want with me?"

"Well there are a lot of things I want, but I am here on business. Business before pleasure, you know. Maybe there won't be time for pleasure at all. At least not today. I haven't decided yet. Now sit down or I promise you I *will* hurt you. When is your friend, the ugly blonde guy in the wingtips, coming back? And, more importantly, when is your Hughes Center friend, Matt, coming in?"

"Tell you what, you creepy bastard, I will sit down but only because I want to hear what the hell you are breaking into my condo for. What is it? You can't get a date or what? Here, let me call you a dating service. There are better ways to get to talk to women than breaking into their homes or taping them to a bed. But you're a fairly ugly guy, so I can see the problem."

Sunny sat down. The sun shone in through the windows on either side of the French doors. There was the low rpm sound of old Piper Cubs outside towing banners over the beach. She heard children playing on the sidewalk. Everything sounded and looked normal except the man with the zapper and gun sitting in front of her with his legs crossed, on her gold Damask chair, smiling, unperturbed.

"Don't try to engage me, lady. Don't try anything except sitting there and keeping your dirty red lips shut real tight or I'll do the old tape trick on your mouth, arms, ankles and anything else I feel like immobilizing."

"Fuck you," Sunny said as she jumped out of her chair and charged the man holding the gun and zapper.

She jammed her fists into his face as she pushed all of her weight into the high-back chair. She felt some of his front teeth bend inward and heard a snapping sound.

The gun, she thought, and looked down. It had fallen to the floor. She looked at his face and saw his handlebar mustache slide off and come to rest beside the gun. She looked at the place where the mustache had been and saw blood flowing out of the mouth onto her and the beautiful gold chair. Her hands were slippery with blood.

She shook with fear as she pulled back and drove both her fists into his mouth again. She drew back her right hand, wrapped her left around it and smashed them both as hard as she could directly onto the bridge of his nose.

Never give up, Grampaw, she thought. *Never.* It kept repeating in her mind, the low and calming sound of her grandfather's voice. *Never give up, never give up.*

He spit and choked on the teeth and blood as he extended his hands and catapulted her across the room into the kitchen. He stood and cupped both his hands, catching the blood flowing from his nose and mouth as though there were something he could do with it, something proper and therapeutic.

She screamed and felt her vocal chords vibrate in her throat. She kept screaming in short spurts and filling her lungs with as much air as she could between the screams. It made her dizzy. The man stood up holding his mouth, thick blood running between his fingers.

She screamed again and picked up a stool and threw it at the French doors. It hit the center of the frame support and nothing happened.

When she felt her vocal chords straining again, she pictured in her mind a slow-motion Road Runner cartoon. There was a full movie screen filled with the Road Runner's vocal chords bouncing up and down. Wet and red throat skin vibrated in the cartoon of her mind and little throat bumps of skin tried hard to swallow when there was too much fear to create saliva.

When the cartoon stopped, she felt herself trying to scream again but nothing came out. Something felt broken in her throat. She stood up and grabbed the knife she had slammed onto the table.

She turned quickly and looked at the man standing in front of the doors. He was backlit with the bright sun filtering through the sheer curtains. He had a look of amazement and disbelief on his face. He shook his head and strings of red and white liquid flew from side to side, like a great dog frothing in the heat of the sun. When he tried to breathe, little red bubbles blew and popped out of his mouth and nose.

Sunny dove to the gun and zapper beside the chair. She picked up the gun and aimed it at him. She felt her index finger tighten on the trigger. She couldn't breathe and the light coming into the room on the bright sunlit summer day turned dark on the edges of her mind. Her peripheral vision narrowed. She was in slow motion again but there wasn't any cartoon playing, just a dark and slow restriction of her vision. Her finger rested on the trigger, trying to squeeze like it was a camera and you had to remember not to jerk it. The picture had to come out clear and if the camera or trigger was pulled too abruptly, there would be a movement at the moment of exposure or, in this case, detonation.

She squeezed and nothing happened. She squeezed harder as the walls of darkness closed in around her.

41

Wolfe appeared in the doorway with two small white bags in each hand, "Hotdoggidy" written in large, bright red letters. Sunny looked at him, her hands frozen on the gun, her finger still on the trigger. Her eyes were large and round like a deer in the night woods, a spotlight freezing it in time and space, a picture on the wall of reality.

"My, my, my, does this bring back memories," Wolfe said. "I do love the smell of gunpowder and pussy in the morning, but I don't smell any gunpowder."

Sunny's eyes looked from the sight on the gun to Wolfe's smiling face. He held the bags higher displaying them like he went to the forest and returned with game. "Cinnamon rolls, anyone?" he said to a now angrier and more frightened Sunny.

She stopped shaking and pointed the gun directly at him. "What, you filthy, is the matter? Your talk. Filthy!" she said.

Wolfe turned toward the kitchen and walked past Sunny and the gun. "More coffee?" he asked.

She screamed and heard squeaky spurts of sound come out as she slammed the gun beside the cinnamon rolls on the counter.

"How dare you be so dirty. You have no respect. I had no idea what a slob you were, you dirty-minded FBI has-been."

Wolfe smiled and walked to one of the oak cabinets in the kitchen. He took out two plates, came back to Sunny and asked her to move. "I need a fork and knife. You're in front of the utensil drawer, bitch."

She didn't move. He nudged her with his hip. She lost her balance and stood looking at him in amazement.

"Shepherd would never have such an obnoxious, incipient, underbred friend," Sunny said. "Is this the way you start all your relationships?"

Wolfe walked over to the wagon wheel coffee table Sunny's grandfather had made. He put the two cinnamon rolls and coffee down on the glass top. "Not shaking anymore, are you, young lady? I'm not ignorant, I'm not a chauvinist, I seldom ever swear, I have hallowed respect for women, especially for you, from all the things I've heard from Matt and Shep."

"Right, oh yeah, right," Sunny said. "I think the real you just came bubbling to the surface, Wolfe Man. And no wonder they call you Wolfey. Creepy FBI spook."

"Sunny, sit down and have a coffee and cinnamon roll." Wolfe kicked his wingtips off. "Sweaty in those things without socks. Listen, Sunny, you aren't crying, shaking, or in some kind of state of shock from some apparently terrible thing that necessitated you pulling a gun on someone. You were ready to snap when I walked into that door and the only reason I became Mr. Garbage Mouth was to distract you. You are distracted, aren't you?"

"Yes."

"Well, it worked, didn't it? It usually does and both Shepherd and I have used that tactic with a few rookies in our time. Only thing is, you have to know what will piss the person off when they're in that condition. I just guessed you had a lot of respect for yourself and by the time I was disrespectful to you, you'd probably blow your pretty top and get angry and become distracted enough to move on."

"Are you serious?" Sunny said.

Wolfe slid over closer to her and stuck his square chin up close to her. "Go ahead," he said. "Hit me. But please, not too hard. I was just trying to help you."

Sunny threw her cinnamon roll on the coffee table and started to wind up for the strike. Wolfe closed his eyes then opened them and looked directly into hers.

Sunny lowered her hand and put her head down toward her cupped hands. She took a deep breath and said, "I'm sorry. I mean, I didn't hit you. I just...."

"Want to talk about it now or later?" Wolfe said.

42

Sunny's phone rang. She remained sitting and looking at her hands as though some answer, some deep and introspective solution, would soon appear there. Wolfe handed her coffee and the cinnamon roll. She hesitated, then took it.

"Good sign," Wolfe said.

Sunny's cell phone rang. Wolfe picked it up. "Hello?"

The voice on the other end was breaking in and out with static interruptions and some dead air.

"That you, Matt? You're breaking up."

"I'm only about a half hour out on the Golden State Parkway. Tell Sunny they found Dr. Fowler. She'll know who I'm talking about. He's okay. He wandered off again and the shrinks have confirmed he does have dissociative fugue, stress-induced. Said at first they thought it was some weird thing called TGA, transient globular amnesia. See you in a short."

Wolfe looked at Sunny munching on the roll and sipping the steaming coffee from a Hughes Center mug. She looked like a little girl to him, one who had skinned her knees and now, with cookies and ice-cold milk, was just fine. *Doesn't take much to get little girls and good women back on their feet,* he thought.

"Sunny, what is this stuff about some kind of fugue and Dr. Dowler? A fugue is a musical thing the last time I looked."

"It *is* a form of music composition," Sunny said. "But more than that. And the only reason I know something about it is that I had a kid hand in a term paper on it. He kept giving me all this grief in what was otherwise a wonderful English class of really bright kids. But he kept making problems to the point that all I did was interrupt our learning to deal with him. I knew he was a nut about music and in a moment of weakness, I made him do a short research paper on fugues."

"Why a moment of weakness? What?"

"It was a moment of weakness, Wolfe, because I don't like to use academics, research and that sort of thing as a punishment. I'd like to use it more as a reward. It defeats the entire purpose if I use it to punish. But what's it matter now? Anyhow, get it?"

"I think."

"This kid got so interested in other forms of music he started playing the cello. Music soothes the savage classroom problem, I guess. But it really did help.

"Anyhow, in a musical fugue there are a number of parts. Each part or voice enters in turn but at different times, as I recall. Then they go on to repeat themselves. They are written for orchestra, chamber music, chorus, all sorts of music media. They're usually for keyboard performance; you know, piano and organ are common. What the heck this TGA thing Matt mentioned to you, I never heard of. Transient globular amnesia? Figure that one out."

"But why the fugue? I mean why the name? I don't get it."

"In dissociative fugue, there are one or more episodes of amnesia and the one afflicted can only recall some of their past, sometimes nothing. And, like in the music, it starts of as one thing and ends up another type of music, or person, whatever the case may be. They actually lose their identity, become a new person and it usually is precipitated by traveling away from home. Weird, I know. Stress can bring it on, too. It's like you start off as one thing, as one person, lose part of it, start another part, become someone else, and it goes on from there. You could be a brain surgeon and end up working as a farmhand building your whole life all over.

"Think about it, Wolfe. If you're an expert, a rocket scientist or something and you get this disease, what good would you be to the people who wanted information from you? Hell, they may as well let you go. But the problem with that is, the disease can go away in hours, weeks or months, sometimes longer."

Sunny stood up, wondering how fast life was changing— from a gun to coffee and rolls to fugue to amnesia.

She took the two cups, plates and utensils to the kitchen counter. She opened the dishwasher and stuck them in. Gun to dishwasher to soap pellets to broken teeth attack. What next?

43

Sunny was on the couch with her forearm resting on her head, covering the sunlight shining through the windows. She was in and out of sleep in that land where you wake and are not sure of day or night or if you're supposed to be getting ready for work or vacation.

It was Tuesday and tourist traffic was increasing outside her front door on Beach Drive. Motorcycles, sports cars, and old men on motor scooters passed by, leaving their distinctive sounds, intermingling with her dreams and daydreams, adding an audio to the tinted color she watched pass through her half-conscious state.

Wolfe was on the front deck, his feet propped up on the railing, sound asleep, mouth hanging open, drying in the sun, a coffee cup perched neatly on top of his large bare stomach.

Matt walked up the steps, tiptoed past Wolfe and gently opened the French doors that entered directly to the living room of Sunny's condo. He walked over to her and knelt down. She was sound asleep.

He got back up and walked to a blue leather recliner beside the fireplace. He sat down, tilted back, took a deep breath and closed his eyes.

He opened them when he heard the front door bang against the brass stop that was screwed to the floor. He jumped up at the same time Sunny did to see Shepherd standing in the doorway, the curtains billowing out over him from the 40-miles-per-hour gusts blowing in from the afternoon ocean thermals.

"You scared us," Matt said. "What the hell is the matter with you, making an entrance like that?"

"What's the matter with *me,* you say? What is this red stuff on the floor here? And why is everyone asleep like a bunch of bums at one o'clock in the afternoon?"

Wolfe walked in holding his empty coffee mug and stood behind Matt dry washing his face, forcing his eyes open.

Sunny walked over to the kitchen area and Wolfe to the dining. They each picked up the throw rugs that were soaking on top of the red stains of blood left by the intruder.

"Here's what we've been up to," Sunny said. "Where you been, glamour boy?"

For the next half hour Sunny and Wolfe explained about the intruder. For a few minutes when Sunny was in the middle of her explanation of the attack, she started to tense up. She felt the anger begin to overtake her, wrap her in the fearful nonsense of life and death and the potential of it all. She looked at Wolfe and stopped in the middle of her sentence. He walked over to her, put his hand on her trembling shoulder and whispered in her ear, "Don't make me say bad things to such a nice lady. I don't want you to hear me swear for another decade or two."

She laughed, stood up and extended her right hand to him. He stood and hugged her. She said, "Thank you, Wolfey."

Matt walked around the plastic drop cloth that Sunny had thrown over some of the bloodstains. "Well, we've all really had a lot happen," he said. "Too soon, too quick, too fast, too much. Where do you start?"

Sunny walked over to the dining room table, grabbed it and dragged it toward the living room. Shepherd and Wolfe got up, went over to Sunny, picked it up and placed it in front of the fireplace. Matt watched from the couch. "Nice of you to help out, big boy," Sunny said.

"I'm sorry, I wasn't thinking," Matt said. "Mind was somewhere else."

He attempted to carry one of the chairs from the dining room and stepped on top of the plastic covering the blood.

"Matt, do you mind? I have it soaking. It'll probably never come out anyhow."

"Ah, sorry," Matt said. "I mean sorry, again, or something. I don't know."

Sunny looked at him and shrugged her shoulders. They took their drinks to the table and sat down.

"Here's how it is," Matt said. "I know I'm kind of a klutz. I know I don't keep my body and my mind in the same place at the same time. But we have to put this all together and—"

The others in the room raised their arms in a simultaneous motion for Matt to stop. Sunny said, "Not another lecture, Matt. Please."

A soft, hot wind came in from the ocean. The sun was high in the sky and bodies were still turning red on the beach. They looked out at the passing joggers, cars and hot dog venders. Sunny folded her hands and looked down at her lemonade. “Sure doesn’t feel like being at the beach anymore. Not feeling much of anything good at all.” She looked up at the men gazing at her. “Maybe I’m running with the wrong crowd. Maybe I need some different friends.”

They kept looking at her, no one hearing the sounds of life outside.

“Just kidding,” she said. “But you guys do have to come up with something. I just teach English.”

44

Shepherd stood and stretched. "When I was in the Yucatan Peninsula back in '83," he said, "there was a woman with large sums of money and property who showed great interest in me."

Wolfe interrupted. "And when I was in Georgetown in '84, there were five poor women who looked to me for emotional, erotic and financial sustenance." They both laughed and sat back down, each reaching in their pockets and taking out Palm Pilots. Matt took out an IPAQ and each man pushed buttons. Beeps and dots and dashes filled the room.

Sunny looked at them. *Men and their toys,* she thought. She chewed on an ice cube and swirled the remaining liquid and disappearing cubes in her glass in hopes of accelerating the melt rate to get something cold down her throat. She gave up and headed for the refrigerator.

Matt stood up and took the glass from her hand. "I'll get it. You sit. Beer?" he asked.

"No, Matt. Lemonade. Pay attention," she said. "What is it with me? It's like this terminal irritability about all this and that. I snap at Matt. I look outside and see sunshine but don't feel any inside. I see children and families and happy people and they are distant, way out there somewhere in another place away from where I am."

Matt put the lemonade in front of her. "You *are* edgy," he said. She looked up at him with displeasure.

Shepherd said, "Oh, boy. Maybe we better just move right along."

"See, you didn't do anything and I'm looking at you like I could scream or cry and I don't know which," she said.

Shepherd put down his Palm Pilot and said, "Look what you've been through, Sunny. Your grandfather, the man who loved and raised you, dies. Then your grandmother. Then this stuff."

"This stuff," Sunny said. "Stuff? This is amazing. This approaches unreality to me. A month ago I was teaching *The Canterbury Tales* and today I'm fighting off…I don't know what I'm fighting off. It is a far cry from English class and working out on a sunny morning beach. I mean, really, look at it all. There's this feeling like some catastrophic thing is going to jump out at all of us before it ends. Like I'm forgetting something all the time, like I didn't turn the coffee maker off and I left for Asia and somewhere over the Pacific I remember but there's nothing I can do."

Sunny looked at the three men at the table, each one pushing buttons on their Palms and IPAQs, periodically glancing at each other and pointing to an icon, shrugging their shoulders.

"Nice to have a concerned audience," she said.

Matt looked up from his Palm device. "Ask me anything," he said. "I heard every word you said. Coffee worries, Asia, Pacific, meaningless sun and exercises void of the glucose rush you would normally feel. See, I was listening."

Wolfe looked up from his device. "Yeah, I'm looking at a website here. Maybe existential void depression. Maybe delayed from your grandfather dying then all this happening."

"No," Shepherd said. "Not existential. I don't see it. Not according to what I'm reading on this one. She knows who she is, what she is, what her plans are, where she's going. We're not talking existential here. And look, look at us all together. She has friends who care. And there's Matt. Well, maybe there's Matt."

"How about some eye contact? Play with your toys later?" Sunny said. "You're not going to find me in your little beeping boxes.

"I've been attacked by some prince of fucking darkness, master-of-disguise bastard who broke into my condo and pulled a gun and electronic zapper on me. Why'd he come in here? Where'd he come from, and is he coming back? He didn't get to the part about telling me why he was here. I shoved some of his teeth down his throat. And that was nothing but luck and stupid fear that he just didn't expect from me.

"Then there's the disgusting plastination art in the corner of that deli apartment in the Strip in Pittsburgh. And there's the crashed 767 and the dithering device codes missing and the CDs from the guy's place and the collocated antennas and model planes that could carry e-bombs. Then there's poor Clark Dowler's fugue…ah, amnesia thing. For all I know, he's the wacko after me. Probably forgot who he was—is.

"And all this has to fit together before more planes crash and buildings are constructed with incorrect coordinates and ships don't mess up because of slightly off GPS coordinates that land them in a foggy ocean crossing with thousands of people onboard, and…"

"Let *me* say," Matt said. "And I lost my job and used a government jet without permission from The Shark and I'm begging to get the job back and she, the Friggin' Egomaniacal Shark, wants to crawl in the sack with me, or anyone for that matter, and I think I already have a girlfriend sitting at this table. At least I think I do."

"Can we take out our palm devices again?" Shepherd said. "I'd like to take notes and you've put we technologically addicted men here at a disadvantage. These devices have new Word programs, state of the art software called 'HOW TO HANDLE WOMEN IN STRESS WHO ARE DOING WELL AND DON'T REALIZE IT.'"

There was forced laughter from the table. Everyone stopped moving; Palm Pilots and IPAQs glowed unattended on the table.

Matt reached over and put his hand on Sunny's wrist. There was an electrically charged and awkward silence as Shepherd and Wolfe looked at Sunny and Matt. Hear no evil, see no evil, use no Palm Pilot.

Wolfe said, "Maybe you could get your job back after all, Matt. Why not compromise? Use your body on The Shark but by all means use *my penis*. Admittedly there would be some foreplay you'd have to put up with, but not sex by any definition. Look at Bill-Boy Clinton. Hell, you'd have it made."

There was a moment of silence then laughter. Matt put his hands in front of Sunny to give her the opportunity to stand up close to him. She did and they hugged for the first time since their missed date, for the first time since seeing the horrible art, the crashed 767 on the news, and model aircraft capable of crossing the Atlantic and carrying e-bombs.

Shepherd and Wolfe put their Palm Pilots away, voluntarily. "Maybe we better go into the other room. Maybe talk later," Wolfe said.

Somewhere out on the beach a child looked up at the Piper Cub towing the sign about evening entertainment at the Lobster Festival. He pointed and jumped up and down, screaming for his parents to look. He'd never seen a plane towing a banner before. His mother and father, both sound asleep, stirred and repositioned their red bodies on beach blankets.

"And look, Mommy. Look at the little model plane coming behind it. Shouldn't it have a sign too? Just a little one?"

45

“Is it paranoia, double vision, or my over-sensitized nervous system?” Shepherd asked Wolfe. They were on the front deck giving Matt and Sunny some private time alone. “Do you see one old gray Cub towing a sign or do you see one gray Cub and a radio-controlled model behind it?”

“For the sake of all that is right, Shep, don’t get your gun. Don’t shoot anything. Don’t call the guard or your old boss at the Bureau. Let’s just go out and throw rocks at it. It can’t be more than fifty feet off the deck.”

“Are we both nuts?” Wolfe asked. “I’m starting to think we have more of an adjustment and post-traumatic stress thing going here than Sunny does. Do you think tossing little rocks at some toy is going to help us? Why not just start blowing up every model airplane shop in the tri-state area? Makes about as much sense.”

“Let’s follow it,” Shepherd said. “The plane is going to parallel the beach the rest of the way to Wildwood, Avalon, Stone Harbor and Atlantic City. I know it is ridiculous and probably nothing, but if there is in fact an e-bomb or dirty bomb on that little thing, it could blow the Cub and the poor soul on board into little pieces.”

They went inside and saw Sunny and Matt on the couch looking into each other’s eyes, no e-bombs or dithering of GPS signals on their minds.

Wolfe went over to the kitchen table and picked up Matt’s keys to the Rent-A-Wreck. He walked outside, closed the door gently and headed to the parking lot. The Wreck was in D-43 where Matt had left it. As they approached, Wolfe looked at Shepherd and said, “What if the plane is a hot bomb and what if it is being controlled by the guy in the Cub? I mean the pilot isn’t the victim, the pilot has the control mechanism for the radio-controlled drone with the bomb? Maybe?”

"So, what are you saying?" Shepherd asked. "We shoot down both, throw rocks at both, or what?"

They didn't speak. They got in the car and turned right onto Ocean's One then made another right and went left on Beach Drive. Wolfe drove and Shepherd rode shotgun, periodically sticking his head out the window to keep the Cub and the drone in sight.

The car kept up to the slow-flying Cub. And two grown men squinted into the bright beach sun, losing sight of their tow plane and the radio-controlled drone, all alone and both wondering if they were crazy or wise or stupid but at the same time not caring how they appeared to the rest of the world.

"Ya know what?" Shepherd asked. "What can we do if we stick with this thing anyhow? It'll end up back at Cape May County. Won't it? I mean, is that the home base? Is that where they hook the signs, unhook them, get other signs, fuel up?"

"Yeah, I guess," Wolfe said. "Let's wait at the airport. Get the N number off the thing so we know which one of those old ugly Cubs we're looking for."

"Once we get it what are we going to do with it? I seriously doubt that a radio-controlled model is going to land in tandem with the Cub. Like it's going to sit there and we're going to dismantle it looking for the tech bomb or dirty Molotov."

He turned away from the Cub and the little escort tucked in neatly behind it. It buzzed along above the populated beaches with boys and girls and mums and dads turning red on the hot burning sand.

46

Tom Sheldon loved the way the ocean wind blew into the open door and window of the J-3 Piper Cub. He showed up for work each day in shorts, a T-shirt, and baseball cap. There was no tie to wear or suit with uncomfortable shoes. Hell, sometimes he kicked off his tennis shoes and flew in bare feet. It helped him feel cooler on the exceptionally hot days.

The wind, the sun and the grass strip he took off from each day were like home to him. The smell of fuel, the laughs with mechanics and other young pilots made him feel alive and he sometimes wondered if he shouldn't just do the banner towing for a living, follow the weather up and down the east coast. Maybe do the towing in Miami when there was no work in the Northeast. Maybe do more flight instruction in the off hours. Besides, he'd heard about the jet going down in Pittsburgh.

But there wasn't much money in flying old fabric and tube Cubs above the beach all day. And flight training was very expensive, especially when it was time to get a multi-engine rating or turbine time so he could qualify to apply for the airlines.

That's why he listened to the charming man with the long black hair, the stupid-looking Hitler mustache and the missing front teeth. When he talked to him, he wondered why such a nice guy would have one of those dirty square things growing under his nose, especially when it seemed to draw more attention to the cuts and stitches on his lips. The guy even had a hard time talking, especially with the speech impediment. He'd talk, or rather try to talk, and then he'd stutter, say one or two words, then have to slap his knee or touch his head before anything came out without a struggle. It was like this imaginary button moved all over him and he had to find it, push it, and then he could say a few words without stuttering.

Sheldon didn't care what the man looked or sounded like. He didn't care about the ridiculous amount of cheap cologne he wore. He remembered his mother telling him if someone has to wear a lot of perfume or cologne they are hiding something. *This guy needed to hide,* he thought. He was a mess. But the badly needed money was more important than what he might be hiding.

That's why when the guy told him he wanted to play a practical joke on a friend and fly a model airplane onto his front lawn towing a sign that said, "WILL YOU MARRY ME? LOVE YOU, SUNNY—MATT," Sheldon agreed.

It was so easy. Take the $150 dollars cash, get to within a quarter mile of the condo and let it loose. It was on the flight path of the banner route, anyhow.

Sunny and Matt, he said, were friends of his and when he was visiting them for breakfast he put a homing device in the yard, right in front of their deck. Naturally Matt knew all about the surprise, but Sunny didn't have a clue. The plane couldn't land, of course, but it could crash and Matt would stay inside and Sunny would go out and see the plane, walk over to it and realize it had a tail on it with a message. That's when she'd pick it up and read the marriage proposal.

There was supposed to be an engagement ring in the cockpit too, just a cheap one, a substitute. Then Matt would give her the real one later. And the weird guy told him also that there was "something else in there that would really get their attention."

47

They were becoming closed in by the walls and the constricting conversation about relationships, responsibilities, loyalty and love. It encircled them and bound them up, forcing them artificially close to one another. It was like enjoying night stars together with your lover but looking at the ground instead of up where billions of miracles twinkled.

Sunny said, "Why are we sitting here talking about our relationship, the problems, the future? What is this all about, anyhow? What is the point to talk? There's an ocean out there, Matt, and sky and sun and life happening and you and I have to save the world. Is that our job? Who the hell are we to be so arrogant to think we can do something? I'd say we are over our heads with our crew here. I mean, we have two overweight, retired Feds, an English teacher and a tech from the Hughes Center. There are three men and two of them have handled, at least I think they have, some serious problems in their careers. And who is it that gets their house broken into and has to defend her dignity and her life? Oh yes, then there's Carl, our absentee resident in morbid topics. I think we need to be sitting on the beach or in a five-star gourmet restaurant or something more that speed. We give this to the authorities and we take a hike."

Matt looked at Sunny, blank and pale from too little sleep and too much worry. "Let's see," he said. "We should quit what we're doing and go back to business as usual? That's what you're saying? There's a point of no return on things, Sunny. Like once you start down the sliding board or waterfall, you can't change your mind."

"You think you're a philosopher," Sunny said. "Well, let me think a minute, Matt. No, not a philosopher—a consumer. That's it, a consumer who likes high-tech stuff and Palm Pilots instead of listening to his, and I am starting to use the term loosely again, his girl. Come on. See what happens when we talk?

We need to live. Let's go outside and watch the day—live a little, damn it."

They walked onto the deck together, stood at the top of the steps and felt the wind whip around the corner of the condo. Matt put his arms around Sunny and Sunny puckered her lips, made a face and shook her head. Her hair blew out of control and a few strands stopped around her eyes where there was moisture. "Oh, what the hell," she said. "Nobody is perfect. And I'll tell you, Matt. Sometimes I'm no prize. Maybe you've noticed."

Matt looked down at her and pulled the hair out of her eyes. "Your eyes are wet," he said. "That's why your hair got stuck there."

"Wow. You are an observant one," Sunny said. "And so very romantic."

"I get it. You're crying, aren't you, Sunny?"

They hugged the second time since the missed date, the dithering, plastination, deli apartment, and the 767 crash at PIT, Matt's new job problem and Sunny's attack.

Matt held her and some kids on skateboards whistled and yelled from the boardwalk opposite Beach Drive. Matt waved at them and smiled. "I'm really sorry about you getting attacked, Sunny," he said. "Wait. I have that wrong. That is to say, I'm sorry you had to attack the intruder. Poor bastard has to be hurting."

Sunny smiled. "I'd say he's probably spent some time in the dentist's chair."

"No," Matt said. "I'd say he's been in to see an oral surgeon."

They laughed and sat down on the wicker love seat. Matt took off his shirt and spread his arms to the sky, a free bird spreading his wings, waiting for magic to take him away. The wind picked up the shirt and blew it three condos down. He let it go. "This feels great, Sunny. You are right about stopping and remembering to enjoy life, smelling the flowers or whatever it is you want to smell."

The radio-controlled model turned sharp left. The Cub continued straight on course in the direction of Wildwood, Avalon Beach, Stone Harbor and Atlantic City, spreading messages about food and entertainment and spectacular prices.

Sunny heard the high-pitched tone of the RC model as it crossed the hot beach, the boardwalk then Beach Drive. It did not slow down; the nose did not pitch up to prepare for a landing or controlled crash in front of the condo. It whined loudly at full throttle at an altitude high enough to go to a pitch-down position that would increase the airspeed to the maximum velocity.

Matt's eyes closed as Sunny stood up and squinted into the sun, trying to make out exactly what was heading for them.

Sunny knew sometimes there were fifty kites on the beach flying their bright colors with sound effects and aerobatics. This sound was different and there were no aerobatics and no strings attached, just a small plane headed for the condo.

Matt reached up and felt for Sunny's hand. His eyes closed as he sensed the moment. He felt her hand compress in his grip. "Come on, sit," he said. "You're the one who said we needed a break. Talk to me. Visit me. Maybe we should go inside for a while. Mess around. You know?"

Sunny reached out and put her fist into Matt's stomach, grabbed his belt and tried to pull him to his feet while she screamed, "Visit, visit, talk, shit, run—I think."

He opened his eyes about the time the RC crossed the sidewalk just in front of the condo, landscaping and yard. The wind turned the nose twenty-five degrees away from Sunny and Matt.

"Look at that thing," Sunny said. "It's compensating for the wind. Heading right at us. How? What the hell is it?"

When Matt's eyes opened he froze in anticipation of impact or detonation or just a stupid mistake being made by a little boy and a radio-controlled toy.

The sound, like a cheap, miniature Texas chainsaw buzz, grew louder as it crossed a swath of yellow and red flowers paralleling the sidewalk in front of the condo. Matt stood, the noise delivering him from a beach day sunny reverie. He staggered and rubbed his eyes. He thought that maybe it was an expensive toy, maybe a mistake, maybe out of control, dead batteries in the control unit, a harmless error in heading…

They stood motionless, in a startled trance, a curious onlooker daydream. What is this curious toy, this technically fun RC plane, this pleasant distraction? They observed the curious plane as though studying the Grand Canyon or dolphins swimming majestically just offshore, or the distant flash of summer lightning. It was an out-of-place tourist attraction until they spotted the canisters. They saw the two small cylindrical containers hanging beneath the wings, each suspended from two wires and bouncing erratically in the slipstream of the radio-controlled model. This was clear. This was fact. This was not a cute plane flown by a careless little kid.

The canisters flipped to the inverted position, spun, and became still for a moment after banging on the underside of the wing. Torn pieces of fabric and wood detached from the wings each time there was a strike.

The aircraft was low and slow and beneath them as they stood on the elevated deck looking down at the thing closing in, now apparently aimed at them or something behind them. They were between the aircraft and the front door of the condo and in their minds, without having to think about thinking or planning a move, they pushed themselves away from the front railing of the deck.

Their minds were working together, survival the only topic in that deep place where body and soul scream *survival* above all else.

Sunny turned to run to the east end of the deck while Matt tried to go west. The plane's nose poked through a gap between two cross rails in the fencing surrounding the deck. Its left and right wings hit simultaneously. The two swinging canisters remained in motion and became projectiles upon impact. The bomb on the right wing detached and struck Sunny's right thigh with an ear-shattering snap and crack. Her leg gave out and she reached down to grab that part of her thigh stinging with pain. She tried to tuck and fall into a protective roll but felt her shoulder hit the deck with a dead thumping sound. Her head impacted, and the last thing she saw was Matt turning toward the front door, watching the left canister hit the screen and bounce harmlessly to the ground, spin in circles and come to rest.

Matt looked at the unexploded canister then down at Sunny unconscious on the floor. Blood covered her leg. Matt looked for her eyes and, as he squinted in the bright sun to focus, he saw the red liquid flow from beneath her hair.

Matt looked at the canister sitting in front of the doorway. The wind moved it toward him and made a rolling sound like a marble on cement. He stepped back and felt for the railing behind him. The wind stopped and the canister came to rest on a gap in the floorboards.

He climbed over the railing and dropped to the ground. He walked past the front steps, past Sunny and around to the garden shed behind the condo. There was a padlock on it. Leaning against the door was a shovel. He grabbed the shovel, wedged the metal tip of it between the metal of the hasp and popped the screws out of the metal front holding the lock plate. He opened the door and dragged out a rotary push mower. He took both it and the shovel to the front of the condo, carried the mower onto the deck and leaned the shovel against the front door. He started to push the mower over top of the canister. The wind blew it only an inch or two toward Sunny. He continued pushing the mower until the canister was in the center, just beneath the engine. He pushed further waiting to feel a slight pressure as the rubber safety-guard brushed against the bomb. He felt it and continued pushing toward the edge of the deck, away from Sunny.

48

Wolfe was the first to turn the corner and see her on the deck. He saw Matt with the lawnmower. Wolfe stopped for an instant and then walked toward them. He went up the steps and knelt down beside Sunny, pressed a finger to her wrist, feeling for a pulse, and turned to see Matt concentrating on the mower.

Matt focused on the canister beneath the mower. As he approached the edge of the deck, he stopped and considered whether or not to continue pushing it over.

"Matt?" Wolfe said calmly in the way people do who have been subjected to gunshots, imminent explosions and violence in general. "What are you doing with the mower?"

"Think there may be an explosive device of some kind underneath here, Wolfe. Small one. Maybe same one that got Sunny down there."

Wolfe stood up and walked over to Matt and the mower. "How is she?" Matt said. He was soaked with sweat and it mixed with the salty taste of tears running down his face onto his lips. He licked the salty moisture and kept looking at the mower.

"Don't shove it off the porch. Push down on the handle and lift the mower up. Let me see."

Matt pushed the mower handle down and the front rose up revealing the canister. Without the mower covering it, the gusty ocean wind pushed it along to the next slat in the deck planking. It rolled into the slot and stopped there.

"What the fuck?" Shepherd said as he turned the corner coming from the parking lot.

He dropped two bags of groceries and there was the muffled sound of breaking glass. Matt and Wolfe looked as Shepherd stepped over the bags and hoisted himself onto the deck. He reached into his pocket, took out his cell phone and dialed. He put it back in his pocket and walked toward the mower. As he approached, he saw Wolfe take the mower handle from Matt.

Wolfe bent down, picked up the canister and said, "It's a firecracker, ash can or something. I don't know what they're called. Can't be anything in it, though—too light. Here," he said as he tossed it to Shepherd.

Shepherd caught it, put it close to his face and said, "Something hand-printed here. 'See note inside,' it says."

Shepherd took out a pocketknife, cut an opening and unraveled the thick resin-coated paper. He heard a noise, stopped and looked at Matt kneeling beside Sunny, crying hysterically. Joggers and little children heard him and stopped on the boardwalk. It was the sound of a man and child mixed into one. There was the guttural sort of animal groan and howl, then a childish squeak of compressed throat noises and saliva gurgling.

"Matt," Wolfe said. "She bumped her head when she tripped or something. She'll be fine, for God's sake. And the blood on the leg is from a firecracker, the one that was real. Some powder burns there. This thing here you had under the mower only has a note. Powder was taken out but you can still smell it." He put some of the paper to his nose and walked over to Matt. "Here, smell," he said. "Lighten up, man. Don't panic. Medics will be here in a minute. She's fine. But don't touch her, just in case. Don't move her."

"Oh, I'm sorry," Matt said. "This isn't my thing. I mean, violence—all this stuff. Then again, what have I been through except some run-ins with The Shark?"

Shepherd sat down beside Sunny. Matt and Wolfe sat down on the steps. They heard the sirens above the drone of beach noise, Beach Drive motorcycles, cars and happy screaming kids.

"Yah know, Wolfey," Matt said, "no one sees me on the floor like Sunny over there or finds me dealing with the guy she dealt with. I'm just here for decoration, I think. Don't even have a job, but then again, maybe I do. Existential ambivalence. That's it. Uncertain fluctuation about whether or not I exist."

Wolfe patted Matt on the back. Matt flinched and rubbed his shoulder. "Sorry, Matt, didn't mean it to hurt. Here they are."

The ambulance crew rolled the gurney over, dropped equipment beside Sunny and started to work. Matt stayed on the steps and watched. He saw Sunny jerk her head away from the smelling salts and reach her hand up, ready to strike at a small nurse dressed in a one-piece blue jumpsuit. "She's just fine," one of them said. "Nothing wrong with her except a slight burn and gash on her leg. Hit her head pretty hard, though."

Matt kicked a piece of gravel into the front yard. "Probably will get hit with a mower and put someone's eye out or something," he mumbled.

The crew elevated the gurney and locked it into place at a level where Sunny was in close eye contact with Wolfe, Shepherd and Matt. Shepherd and Wolfe patted her hand. Matt stood there with his hands in his pockets. She didn't speak to Matt as they wheeled the gurney past him toward the steps. Wolfe jumped into the back of the ambulance. Matt went into the house and sat down in the living room. Shepherd went past him into the kitchen and fumbled with the coffee pot. There was some talking outside then the slamming of doors and the sound of an engine starting. There was no siren.

49

At Cape May County Airport, a Piper Cub dropped the sign it had been towing all day. By the time he had flown from Atlantic City the short distance back to Cape May, the weather had gone down to serious black build ups out on the ocean and wind on the mainland. The wings of the old Cub rocked as the young man looped the rope around the tie-down pegs. He pulled to be certain the plane would be there in the morning when he showed up for the next day of flying up and down the coast.

He was alone on the grass landing strip with only one car sitting beside his old Plymouth in the gravel parking lot next to the hangar. The hangar doors were closed. The mechanic had left. The pilots had returned to the field earlier when the weather kicked up into a line of thunderstorms that threatened the entire Northeast. They had also left.

Although there were hours of daylight left, the darkness approached the level that turned on an automatic spotlight at the northeast corner of the hangar. A white misty fog coated everything. It was thick to the point of having a texture, as the pilot walked through the growing moisture toward his car.

He saw the man sitting in the red SUV next to his Plymouth. He recognized the face as the man who had given him the money to play the practical engagement joke with the radio-controlled airplane. He thought maybe something had gone wrong and he wanted his money back. He hadn't been able to see if the plane actually found its target. *Hell, I did what I could,* he thought. He did his part, saw that it got to the general location of the condo, and cut it loose from his control just as he was supposed to.

He felt an anger stirring. His thoughts were on how he was going to pay for the twin-time he needed for his next rating. He couldn't see where there were enough hours in the day to get any more jobs to support himself and pay the money for more training.

The man in the SUV opened the door and extended his hand. The pilot wiped his right hand on his cut-off jeans to get at least the first layer of dirt off. He had been flying all day from the time he checked the oil at 9:30 a.m. to the time he wrapped the frayed rope around the wings and put the plane away for the night. He was young but he was tired.

"Just wanted to thank you," the man said. "And I'd like to give you the rest of the money."

The pilot shook his hand. "The rest of the money? You already paid me. I thought maybe something went wrong and you were going to want your money back."

"Money back?" the man said. "No way. You did an exemplary job. Perfect contact. I might have more work for you. Like to give you a bonus, but a check will have to do. I'm all cashed out."

"Sure," the young man said. "Let's go inside, sit down. I'll get you a pen. Rain is going to be here any minute, anyhow. This is great. Hope she was surprised, you know, I mean the lady that got it, the engagement ring and all."

"Oh, I'm sure she was surprised. I'm sure everyone was. Come one, let's get inside out of the wet."

The pilot dug into his pocket and took out a single key. He wondered why there was no stuttering. He didn't care. He unlocked the door and swung it open. The windowless hangar was completely black inside except for diminishing light that crept in from outside. He headed for a circuit breaker box to the left of the door, next to the office area. The door closed behind him. Both men were in total darkness.

"Oops," the man from the red SUV said. "Dark as a grave. Isn't it?"

50

Matt went over to where Shepherd poured the first cup of coffee from his fresh batch. "Looks blacker than any I've seen for a long time," Shepherd said.

"Yeah," Matt said. "Sunny's isn't ever this black."

Matt grabbed a T-towel hanging from a porcelain towel rack on the kitchen wall. "I'm out of here," he said. "If you go in to see Sunny when Wolfe gets back, I'll go with you. Wait for me."

Shepherd sipped the black coffee. "Wow, really bad, strong," he said. "I think it's bad for my stomach. Where you off to?"

"The gym, Shep. I have to do something to deal with this. I can't think my way through it, can't sleep, can't deal with relationships, and if I'm no good to myself, how can I be good to anyone else?"

"Oh this is bad stuff, man," Shepherd said. "It could hurt anyone who has more than a sip or two."

He poured the remaining coffee from the pot down the drain. He turned to see Matt already out the door, down the steps and onto the boardwalk. He laughed out loud. Cordovan wingtip shoes with nice laces, a T-towel, dress pants and a white shirt. Should make Matt a big hit at the gym. He laughed again and got out a tablespoon measure for the next attempt at coffee.

51

"I can't see shit," the pilot said. "Open the door. Let some light in till I get this breaker on."

There was no answer and the drafty hangar remained black. There was the rattling of old wooden hangar doors that needed repaired, adjusted, replaced. Small rays of light streaked intermittently through the cracks in the walls and between the sliding hangar doors. The holes in the metal building acted as reeds and a thousand whistling noises passed from the outer edges of the structure.

The pilot felt cold with only his tank top on. The perspiration cooled in the darkness and a slight vapor lifted off his shoulders. It reminded him of working construction with his father during summer vacations. They'd be in basements sweating in the heat and as they got hotter, if the temperature and moisture content were right, steam would rise from them and they'd look at each other and laugh.

"Look," he said, "this used to happen to me with my dad when we worked on houses. Hey, you there?"

"Yeah, kid. I'm here. Don't feel good. Think something's wrong with my chest. Something I ate, maybe. Hope it's not my heart. Can you help me? I can't catch my breath."

"Where are you?" the young man asked.

"Here, by the workbench. I think I feel some tools, wires and stuff. And a coat rack. I feel wire hangers, too."

"One second," the pilot said. "I'm almost to the box."

When the light snapped on, the place was lit like a flash of lightning had illuminated their black world. Every line and shadow and piece of equipment was perfect and in its place. They were in an antique hangar with old airplanes;

aviation oil; calendars with pictures of young, peachy perfect girls; photos of jets; Air Force posters; and photos of ships at sea.

The young man looked at everything and thought about how poor but how happy he was, being there and smelling the smells and feeling the hot and cold and life surrounding him.

"Over here," the voice said. "Yeah, it's a bench and coat rack."

The pilot slicked his wet, blonde hair back out of his eyes and moved across the hangar toward the man leaning across the wooden workbench. When he got there, the man was standing straight up, reaching into his pocket. "Here, my checkbook. I think it's just I ate something for lunch that didn't agree. No way I'd be having a heart attack. No way, the shape I stay in."

The pilot felt awkward about being right there while the check was being made out to him. He didn't want to appear anxious to see the amount, but he'd seen the car the man drove, the way he dressed and acted, and he knew how generous the first check was. He couldn't complain about a second check, no matter how much it was. A fat check to be part of flying a radio-controlled plane to a condo so a guy could propose to his girl and offer an engagement ring in an unforgettable manner. What could the big deal be? Some people had more money than brains.

"Here, this enough?" the man said as he slid the check in front of the pilot.

It was the instant he looked into the man's eyes before he looked at the check. The eyes kept him from bothering to look, as though it was pointless to see numbers because something was about to happen to make the amount irrelevant. Everything was irrelevant.

The look wasn't so much a frightening look. Rather, it was that of a determined man with a coolness about him that could only come from having practiced what he was about to do.

And the chemistry, the intimate body-heat chemistry, bubbling over so that anyone who wasn't entirely unconscious could feel the tension building.

The pilot put his hands on the check without looking and slid it off the workbench. He felt the dents and splinters of years of use beneath the soft palm of his hand.

"Aren't you going to look at it?" the man said.

"I'm sure it's fine."

"More than fine, young man. It is generous."

The pilot turned toward the brighter light near the office on the opposite side of the hangar where the main door stood open to the heavy downpour of rain. There was the hard patter and pelting on the metal roof. The ancient sliding hangar doors banged on their stops as the wind increased.

The man leaned on the bench and calmly folded his arms and watched the pilot walk toward the lighted office. He noticed how the young man moved with an athletic grace and confidence. He made a mental reminder of that. The movement, size, and height calculated in his head. Thoughts raced through but didn't startle him because he'd practiced, prepared, lifted tons of weights over the years, smashed those bricks with his fists until calluses deadened his touch.

"Just another job," he mumbled to himself. "Hey, kid, you forgot this."

The pilot stopped and turned, the light reflecting off the musculature of his wet shoulders. "Forgot what?" he said.

"Here," the man said as he headed toward the light.

52

Matt's feet burned as he turned the corner of State and Winston Streets after his mile-and-a-half walk to the gym. He opened the metal and glass door of the entranceway and tripped over a cheap imitation of a Victorian rug. It was supposed to add an air of ambience. It was frayed on the edges from constant wear. There were observable accumulations of white sand where it was worn to the threads.

There was a metal school desk where a fat man in a T-shirt punched numbers into a calculator. Beside him stood a young lady, twenty-five or so, with short black hair. She wore heavy makeup and skintight shorts over black leotards. She looked like she believed she was aerobic instructor of the year.

Rededication of purpose, Matt thought. *Workout, cardio, resistance, and, in other words, declare war on my old self.*

"May I help you, sir?" the young lady asked. She walked around the desk and extended her hand to Matt. "I'm Margie. We have some specials if you'd like to join. Or, maybe you'd like to pay by the day until you see if you like our facility. It is the best in town, you know. Actually, we *are* the only exercise facility in town unless you want to count the kooks who go to the beach at five in the morning and stretch."

She stood too close to him and when she looked up into his eyes it was intentional, too forced.

In the background, Matt caught glimpses of men and boys in muscle shirts with perpetually confident smiles on their faces. He wondered if they slept with smiles. They grunted and strained as they lifted weights that were obviously too heavy for their frames and physical makeup.

"Sir," the lady in tights said as she took him by the arm and pressed his elbow against her breast. "This way. Let me show you what I have."

Matt limped when he felt the pain in his right foot. He felt his body getting cold from the air conditioning. He tried to picture himself working out in wingtips and a dress shirt. He tried to picture himself in shorts and a muscle shirt pumping iron with the boys.

She took him into where the weight lifters were handling the free weights. They walked past them toward the Nautilus and Cybex equipment. Matt looked into the mirror that filled the wall facing the free weights. He stopped, sat down in a metal chair and took his right shoe off, then his sock. There was blood on his toe. He took his other shoe off and looked at that foot. There was no blood, just the beginning of calluses and toenails that needed cutting.

He looked at the lady in tights, her glassy blue eyes, perfect hair, makeup and her constant consciousness of how she looked walking, sitting, talking—demonstrating.

He put his socks and shoes back on and when she turned around from adjusting some weights on the triceps machine to look at Matt, he was already out the door into the heat of Cape May.

"In shape, my ass," he mumbled as he felt the pain in his feet.

53

His right hand was extended, holding something, but the pilot couldn't see what he had; couldn't imagine what he'd forgotten.

With the check in his right hand, he took two steps toward the man, the way people do out of courtesy.

When they were within reaching distance, the young man had the quick reflexes to raise the hand holding the check. He saw the object flying toward him and heard the swishing noise it made cutting through the thick hangar air.

The coat hanger first hit his hand and the sharp sting of pain startled him, made him clasp his wrist with the left hand. As he held the hand he felt the next blow, a much more solid hit, smash against knuckles.

The pilot stood with his feet spread in an instinctive search for balance, but he felt wobbly from the pain. He stepped back, still holding his smashed wrist, all the time watching the eyes of the man in front of him.

As the man came toward him with the coat hanger in one hand and a hammer in the other, the pilot put his right foot behind him and extended it directly into the attacker's groin.

It was a palpable hit. The man dropped the hanger and grabbed his crotch, moaning, trying to hold onto the hammer. His brow wrinkled and his face contorted into a grimace of pain. When he dropped the hammer, he took a few steps backward trying to recover some strength and clear the cobwebs of pain from his head. He then lunged toward the young man with the coat hanger at shoulder level.

When they hit the cement, the pilot was on the bottom, the coat hanger pushing into his throat. He looked into his attacker's eyes and saw the calmness of an accountant or butcher taking care of business with not a thought of violence in them. It was business as usual, maybe the rush of trying to be on schedule or the promise to a client to do a good job on their taxes or offer the best cut of beef.

But he didn't give up to the weight of the body on top of him. He took his painful hands and tried to hit the man's face, sacrificing pain or maybe a deformed hand to win life for another day.

The attacker caught the hands. He raised them as far as they would extend and smashed them down hard onto the cement. He felt them change shape in the grasp of his hands and bend with each forceful hit to the floor.

The pilot felt the pain and the change of form. His head was turned to the side, his ear pressed against the floor. He heard the amplified rustling, rubbing sound of sandpaper on oak, the same sound he heard in another life, a safer life with his father, as his head rolled and scraped across the gritty hangar floor.

As darkness shrouded his consciousness, he felt his head smash to the floor, then the pull of his hair to poise it a few inches above the cement, then a thrust downward for another splat of electrified pain. The part of the pilot, the part of all pilots that says never give up, never quit, made him disobey his body as it cried for the comfort of quiet and submission, begged for the darkness to take him.

He expanded, held his failing breath and made himself tense and stiff under the weight of the body on top of him. He felt the body crawl up closer to his neck, pinning his shoulders to the cement, the knees digging into his shoulders making him helpless, immobile, and at the mercy of the hanger the man held in his hands.

The never-give-up, never-give-in mode kept screaming into the psyche of the fading light surrounding him as he lifted his head to the man's crotch, opened his mouth and bit down with his last glimmer of strength.

There was an echoing scream throughout the hangar and the wind seemed to stop as though listening for the impending end to a battle for life.

The pilot opened his mouth, moved it to where he felt more meat and bit down again with his last bit of strength.

The man on top felt the ripping pain in his crotch. When he opened his mouth to scream, he felt the wound Sunny had given him re-open and flow down onto the pilot who rested motionless on the hangar floor, his jaws clenched in death like a great mastiff refusing to give up his prey.

The bleeding man looked around in the dim light, kneeling on the dead man's shoulders, unable to move, unable to stop the free flow of blood from his mouth or his crotch.

The passionless eyes the pilot had seen earlier in his attacker had disappeared. They were replaced by those of a desperate man unable to believe his state of body and mind, being victor and victim simultaneously. They were the eyes of a survivor, but now a survivor at great cost.

He remained trapped in his kneeling position, turning his head, scanning the hangar, eyeing the workbench tools, trying not to move, fearing the intense pain in his crotch would increase, fearing he would pass out from the pain and be found in a heaping sick pile of pilot, killer, blood and bodies.

He looked at the pegboard holding the neatly hung row of pliers, the tin-snips, clamping devices and saws above the bench. He looked up to see the walls spin and tilt. He chanced to bend gently and low enough to put his hands on the floor and steady himself from the dizzying pain.

His mind worked on the mechanical options to free himself from the dead mastiff jaws of the pilot.

54

Saturday morning Matt woke up at Sunny's condo, alone on the couch and thinking about whether or not his feet might be bleeding on the nice material. Wolfe and Shepherd were on the second floor, each in a separate guest bedroom, and Sunny was on the third floor deck asleep in the hammock.

Matt rolled over when he heard the sound of water running through pipes, a toilet flushing, the heavy footsteps of Wolfe and Shepherd coming down the steps.

"My God, what is she doing up there?" Wolfe said as he fumbled with the coffee maker. "How did your first workout go, Matt?"

Matt threw the blanket off and slowly stood up, looking at his feet. He walked into the kitchen, put his left foot on the stool by the breakfast bar and pointed at it. "Here's how it didn't go, my friend. Not for me. Going to plan B."

Wolfe filled the coffee pot with water from the tap, placed a filter in the maker carefully, and put two handfuls of Mocha Java into it. "And plan B is?"

"Plan B should arrive here this afternoon, maybe later this morning. Overnight shipping, but I'm confident it'll be here in time."

"In time for what?"

"In time to take the place of beating the hell out of myself in a gym with a bunch of grunting animals and leotard-wearing, Spandex women with heavy makeup and asphyxiating perfume."

Shepherd stood in the corner of the kitchen with the toaster above his head. He shook it, moved it closer, and examined the insides as though something was waiting there to be discovered. "It's not toasting," he said. "Nothing glows red in there when I push the thing down. Is the coffee ready yet? I can't think without it."

Wolfe switched the coffee on and took the toaster from Shepherd. He placed it on the countertop and plugged it in. "There, that'll help," he said.

"Pop-Tarts," Wolfe said. "Does she have any Pop-Tarts? Strawberry would be good. Blueberry is okay."

Sunny stood with her hands on her hips, observing the three men in their underwear, desperately trying to manage putting together a breakfast.

"This is beautiful," she said. "True specimens. No, I don't have Pop-Tarts, and no, I don't have bread for toast, and no, I'm not making you guys eggs, and yes, you better get cleaned up and dressed because you aren't buying me breakfast at Uncle Wilber's in your underwear."

"I only need a birdbath," Matt said. "I washed last night after I cleaned up my bleeding feet. I'll use the first floor bathroom."

Wolfe and Shepherd saluted Sunny and went upstairs. Sunny stood as they walked around her. There was a glow about her complexion from the morning sun. She smelled of soap, shampoo and mild perfume. Her spiked hair shined, and when Matt walked past her, he leaned toward it and took a deep, loud inhale. "Beautiful," he said.

She stepped back and said, "Just get dressed. You and the rest of the boys need to get some clothes on."

55

Sunny waited on the deck while the boys got ready for breakfast. The door of Carl Farnley's condo opened. He turned and struggled to hold the screen door, close and lock the front door while holding a cake-glazed donut in his mouth and a briefcase under his arm. His bite had severed the donut and he was worrying about half of it falling.

The briefcase fell. He picked it up, rescued the donut, turned around and headed for his car.

"Carl," Sunny said. "You're up early for a man of leisure. And on Saturday? This isn't like you."

Carl didn't smile. "Got that right. Son-of-a-bitching murder yesterday. Now I have to go jab and poke around at that landing strip where they launch those stupid planes that do the beach advertising."

Carl licked his fingers.

"See you haven't started your Atkins diet yet, have you, Carl?"

"I love these donuts," he said. "Anyhow, one of the young pilots was killed. Really nice guy, they say. Had a great future ahead of him. One of the deputies knew him. Deputy started taking flying lessons from the guy. Hard worker. Waited tables, did some flight instruction, some carpentry and other odds and ends at some of the bed and breakfasts around here to make a few extra bucks for his advanced ratings."

"What happened?"

"You don't want to hear. If you've had your breakfast, Sunny, you'd lose it. Believe me. Anyhow, poor guy is dead, not a clue as to why he was killed, and I'm working Saturday. Bye, have a good day. Remember me at mealtime. Oh, Sunny, see you have some company."

"Yeah," Sunny said. "Just the boys. Believe me. Nothing exciting."

"Matt there?"

"Yeah. I don't want to talk about him."

"Tell him there's a package behind my screen door for him. They screwed up another delivery. It's too big for pornographic material, so I don't have any idea what it is."

"Very funny, Carl. I'll tell him."

Sunny ordered cornmeal pancakes. Matt opted for his two orders of bacon and three eggs, easy over. Shepherd and Wolfe said they'd just eat a little bit of everyone's.

"Not mine," Sunny said.

The breakfast discussions were guarded. Matt concentrated on the bacon and eggs as though it took considerable work to calculate the bites and be certain the last munch on the bacon was done just before or after the last bite of egg.

Sunny divided her pancakes in half and spooned the remaining half onto Wolfe's plate.

"No, no," Wolfe said. "Really, we were just kidding about eating your stuff, Sunny. I don't eat breakfast and my poor friend here, poor Shepherd, has no money. And even though he's hungry, he's tough and will probably last without passing out until suppertime. Then we can just put a dab of sugar or orange juice on his tongue and he'll in all probability come to, maybe."

Shepherd looked at the heavy syrup and layer of grape jelly Sunny had poured over her pancakes. "I wouldn't mind just a smidgen of the pancakes," Shepherd said.

Sunny leaned over the table with her plate and fork. She scraped a good portion of her cornmeal cakes onto the saucer of Shepherd's coffee cup. The saucer was too small to hold them.

"Unauthorized food exchanged," Matt said. "Call condiment security."

Wolfe looked around at everyone and took a large swallow of his black coffee. "We're all being very cute and evasive, aren't we? It's time. It's time to do this thing. Time to catch this guy or go home and forget it."

Matt twirled his last bite of bacon around the plate collecting the last remains of eggs. "I'm ready for anything. Bring the sons-a-bitches on."

"Who are they? Where are they?" Sunny said.

Matt leaned over for another sniff of her hair. "It smells like maple syrup," he said. "No, really. There is only one we know to get and that one was at

Sunny's condo, that one was at the Strip District in Pittsburgh and that same one, I suspect, was in the old hangar at the grass strip Carl's at right now. It's all we have. There's nowhere else to go, no one else to catch, torture or give truth serum to."

Sunny slammed her fork onto the plate. Syrup and pieces of breakfast splashed on the table. "My God, Matt. Why are we sitting here like a bunch of clowns making jokes, being cute? Why the hell aren't we with Carl?"

"I was hungry," Matt said.

"Sunny," Wolfe said. "Carl will be there for hours. There is no rush. We all know that and so do you. You're tightening up again and I don't blame you. Finish your breakfast and we'll drive out there."

Sunny looked down at the mess she'd made. She placed layers of napkins over the splattered areas and smiled. "Sorry," she said. "I'm not a Fed. I'm an English teacher with a plane that has a broken door. No, a missing door, and I'm ready for a vacation."

Matt folded his hands in front of him and put them down on his plate on top of the remains of breakfast #3 at Uncle Wilber's. "Oh my God," he said. "This is sticky stuff. Oh, look. Saved by three layers of napkins I put there while you all were philosophizing. By the way. Could we stop at the condo on the way to Carl's investigation? I think there might be a package there for me."

56

The lunch crowd from the beach stood in their bare feet. Some tiptoed on the hot pavement waiting for their hot dogs from the venders. Wolfe, Shepherd and Sunny watched from the deck, amusing themselves with the built-in entertainment.

On the front steps, Matt stuck a knife carefully into a large box. "This stuff is amazing," he said. "You'll love it."

He slit the seams of the cardboard with the black Swiss Army knife. He folded the shining blade and shoved it into his pocket and pulled out the first item.

"This going to be a sort of show and tell?" Sunny asked.

Matt held up a can of aerosol spray. "Spook spray," he said. "Spray this stuff on an envelope and you can detect contents in terms of powdery substances."

They watched Matt silently. Shepherd and Wolfe shook their heads as though to say, "Don't discourage him. See where he goes with this."

"And these are medical-grade rubber gloves, and a biological, chemical, and nuclear protection mask. It's Israeli. Not many of these babies around. I paid extra. And check this. Beautiful. For mail opening protection, look at this miniature scanner for metal and bombs. And I'll carry this thing—the electrical TASER. Of course there's the pepper mace and the other essentials to carry with you that aren't that obstructive or obvious. And check this—a stun gun that looks like a cell phone. Can you believe this one—625,000 volts?"

"Don't zap your ear by mistake, Matt," Sunny said. "Don't talk into the wrong one and be careful of your lips."

Matt reached to the bottom of the box, still digging into his bag of high-tech tricks. "And a collapsible blowgun," he said. "And here's some handcuffs and plastic leg irons."

"Oh, Matt, you are a savage after all, aren't you?" Wolfe said.

They all laughed except Matt who kept digging in the bottom like a child at Christmas. He pulled out a small cardboard box. "Here, Sunny. It looks like lipstick, but there's a very sharp knife in there instead of the makeup. The lips again. Be careful."

"Lot of discussion of lips here," Wolfe said. "Anything in there for us, Matt?"

"How about bear repellent? I got bear repellent," Matt said as he gave one last sweep of his hands at the bottom of the empty box.

Matt picked up wrapping paper and stowed it into the box. He picked it up and headed for the dumpster behind the condo. Before he turned the corner, Shepherd stood up, extended his arms, stretched and said, "Oh, and Matt. The point to all this stuff is?"

"To keep me from having to work out at that stupid gym."

"And you are going to tote around bear repellent and rubber gloves and all this junk?"

Matt stood at the corner, holding his big box. "Don't be stupid," he said. "I'll only carry the essentials for personal protection. Most will fit in my pockets, my big pockets and photography vest. If there's an overflow, I'll wear a fanny pack."

"You say a funny pack?" Sunny said.

The trip to the landing strip was quick. They drove to the end of Beach Drive, made a left away from the Atlantic, crossed the viaduct, then the inter-coastal bridge, got the Golden State Parkway and took the Rio Grande exit.

The strip was just a mile and a half from the exit. When they arrived, Matt was in the back seat adjusting his fanny pack. "I know I won't need it here. Just trying to get used to it, so don't be looking at me like I'm crazy or something," he said.

They pulled into a dirt parking area. There was an accumulation of dust on three police black and whites, an ambulance, and two unmarked Crown Victorias, the kind you see on the side of the road trying to look innocuous.

Carl Farnley was sitting under the wing of a decaying Piper Cub with his snap-on tie beside him on the tall grass. He was drinking an iced tea from a quart bottle. "Over here," he said when he saw Sunny get out of the driver's side of the car.

They stood around Carl and watched him sip his tea. "Ugly," he said. "Very ugly. Never saw anything like it in my life. Can't believe what some people will do. That pilot really gave a fight, though. And he was smart. Must have been alive when the attacker cut himself loose."

"What do you mean, 'cut himself loose'?" Sunny asked.

Farnley looked at her. "Never mind, young lady. Not important. What's important is what the pilot wrote while he was dying beside the workbench. He wrote it in WD 40—you know, that spray lubricant with the thin red nozzle. It sprays very accurately to get into tight places. Well, he used it to write a note on the wall behind the bench. Kinda messy. Probably couldn't see shit. Poor kid. Usually you can't when you're dying, and considering what he went through, I can't believe he even could think, let alone write."

"He didn't give up," Sunny said. "He'd never give up."

Carl took three gulps of the tea. "What it said was. Well, it doesn't make all that much sense to me. It said, 'impstr'. Go figure. Then there was a circle with an x through it then another with an x through it. You can barely tell the thing is a circle, but if I had to guess, I'd say it is a circle, like a head then the thing is crossed out with an x."

"May I?" Sunny said.

Carl finished the tea and accepted the help from Wolfe, Matt and Shepherd when they offered to hoist him to his feet. "Just don't mind the mess," he said to Sunny. "That's the owner over there, the owner of the strip and planes. Hasn't cleaned up yet. I suspect they'll paint the entire place, rearrange everything. You know, the spirit will still be here. You don't get rid of this type of thing with paint or rearranging workbenches and tools. It becomes part of the lay of the spiritual and eternal land."

Wolfe looked at Carl. "You're so deep," he said.

"Up yours," said Carl.

Matt patted him on the back and said, "And you're versatile, too."

The cold front having passed through the east left that clean and sustained feel of perfection to the atmosphere. The stillness and silence amplified the clicks and clanks of technicians testing and moving and bagging evidence.

"Over there, in front of the workbench," Carl said to Sunny. He looked at Wolfe and Shepherd and said, "You Feds ever get used to this stuff when you worked?"

"Yes," they said simultaneously. Then Shepherd said, "Except some nights when I wake up and the photo in my mind, the color photo, is from twenty years ago and I'm sweating and feel like I need a couple drinks."

"What do you do?"

"Take an over-the-counter sleeping pill, drink a quart of water, and turn on jazz, very low and slow jazz."

"It work?" Carl asked.

"Usually."

Sunny crawled out from under the bench. She'd slid in from the side of the bench and stayed up against the wall to avoid the plastic sheet covering an area directly in front of the work area. "It could be 'impersonator,'" she said. Only reason I'm saying that is pilots who copy instrument clearances in lousy weather have to jot down a lot of information while the control center rattles it off like a machine gun. I mean, it could be lots of other things like, 'impersario, impresario, imperceptions. But look at the imperfect circles. They're a mess but they're heads, human heads, and they're both crossed out and this one has something where the nose would be and this one has nothing where the nose would be. Impersonator?"

"That's a stretch," Farnley said. "And, Matt, where the hell did you find a fanny pack the size of a golf bag? What's in there? Your lunch?"

"No, your lunch, fat ass. Get off my back."

Farnley twisted his face like a child confused when struck the first time emotionally or physically. "Matt, what's wrong?" he asked. "Matt, we're friends. What are you saying to me? This isn't you."

Matt turned away from the group, his head down, looking into the contents of his great yellow and black fanny pack. He plopped down on the grass, a sandbox child organizing, moving pieces in the pack to the special little compartments for quick and easy access.

"He okay?" Farnley asked.

Shepherd flipped his cell phone closed and said, "Yeah, I think. But I don't know for how long. He isn't used to this stuff. Same as Sunny. This call was from The Shark. Something going on at the Center. Wants me there, but only me. Said to keep all you guys away. Piss on her. Let's go, all of you. Catch you later, Carl."

57

The guard at the gate of the Hughes Center was tall and looked impressive in his navy and white uniform. He knew his mother would have been proud and happy because the shining buttons and colorful epaulets signified something. It was a uniform fit for a general's dress wardrobe.

Matt gave a mock salute as the Rent-A-Wreck rocked to a stop beside the gate. "Afternoon, Colonel," Matt said.

Shepherd looked to his left in the back seat at Wolfe and said in a low tone, "What is it with him? All of a sudden a smart ass. Calls Farnley fat ass; smart mouths that harmless, poor guy in the guardhouse. What's next?"

"Maybe The Shark is next," Wolfe said.

"Please, no," he said. "Maybe it's the fanny pack. The new, high-tech-self-defense man. This won't do. You want to snatch it, pitch it out the window?"

The guard didn't laugh and didn't return the salute to Matt. "Sir," he said, "you'll have to step out of the vehicle. The rest of you, too."

"What?" Matt said. "What is this? We never get out of the cars."

The guard unsnapped the leather covering the .44mm Beretta but did not draw it. He looked into Matt's face, then stuck his head near the window and gestured to the others in the car. "As I understand, sir, you're not employed here any longer."

"We're with him," Matt said as he gestured into the back seat where the guard's boss, Shepherd, sat quietly. "Oh, good afternoon, sir, sir," he stammered at Shepherd.

"What's up?" Shepherd said as the guard re-snapped the cover to his weapon.

The guard pointed toward the winding road leading to the main building of the Center. Behind the plate glass windows of the three-story structure there was a cloud of rising smoke. With the windows of the Wreck down, there was a smell of burning plastic in the air. Matt floored the Wreck and the guard pushed himself away from the car. He took two steps back and yelled, "Hey, you forgot your visitor passes."

In the main entrance of the building, they were smothered in an oppressive heat. There was an exaggerated and gagging extension of the plastic they smelled at the guardhouse. It was concentrated and asphyxiating.

Well-dressed secretaries and men in three-piece suits tried to see if there was a way to open a vent or window somewhere in the vast expanse of the building's entrance.

Matt calmly asked them to step back. When they looked at him and continued trying to open windows that were not designed to open, he grabbed two of the men and escorted them to the far side of the room. He propped the front doors open with two red office chairs and shouted across the lobby for Shepherd to give him a hand.

Shepherd jogged over to Matt. Matt sat down in one of the red chairs and asked Shepherd to sit in the other. "You have your piece on you, Shep?" Matt said.

Shepherd pushed back his suit coat and looked down at his small, stainless steel .38mm Colt. "Yeah, here," he said. "Why, feeling particularly insecure?"

Matt reached over and took it out of Shep's shoulder holster. He screamed, "Clear," stood up, took ten steps toward the two-story window, aimed the Colt and pulled the trigger.

"There," he said. "Fresh air."

Anyone in the lobby who was sitting, stood. Anyone who was standing turned and ran toward the open doors where the chairs were propped.

Matt reached into his fanny pack and extracted a digital camera, aimed it at the falling glass and snapped a picture. He then walked toward the cascading glass that flowed like a waterfall and headed for the people who had wisely evacuated toward the front doors. He again reached into the pack and took out a yellow cellophane packet with a nozzle and some printing on it.

As the glass crunched underfoot, he shouted to some secretaries who were coughing and spitting from the fumes. "Share this," he screamed. "Put it over your head and take a couple breaths. Pass it on. Not too many puffs of oxygen in it, but it'll help. Share the puffs."

The three-piece suit guys looked at Matt as he walked around the open-air expanse made by one shot from the .38.

Shepherd stepped across the threshold leading to the courtyard. There were three fountains spraying water into the air, flowers planted in geometric patterns, and brick walkways between ponds with lily pads, bird baths, picnic benches, gazebos and trash cans in the shape of giant mushrooms. There was no hint of glass in the courtyard area. It remained undisturbed as though waiting for the next group of lunchtime employees to sit down and enjoy the artificial scenery.

Matt and Shepherd looked up to the second story where a few sharp, icicle shards of glass hung from the steel support for the second floor.

"It shouldn't have done this," Shepherd said. "There should have been one .38mm slug-sized hole going through that glass and there should have been no shattering whatsoever."

"Yeah," Matt said. "And The Shark isn't supposed to hit on every male within a five-mile radius of her, and no one is supposed to attack government buildings."

58

An elevator bell sounded. Everyone watched The Shark exit the dark interior with two security-types on each side of her. The one on her left put his hand under her arm and helped her over a pile of broken glass. She headed for a coffee table constructed from the wing of a World War II bomber. She let the guard help her the rest of the distance although there were no more footing obstacles to overcome.

Matt and Shepherd came in through the hole that was once a gigantic two-story window. The Shark reached into her purse and took out a cigarette. The guard who had helped her to the couch flicked his Bic. She inhaled deeply, tilted her head up and exhaled toward the face of the other guard. "Why didn't you just have everyone go outside and take a few deep breaths, Matt?"

Matt sat on the coffee table wing so he could face The Shark directly. "The window was a mistake," he said.

The Shark scooted to the edge of the couch and took another drag on her cigarette. She leaned closer to Matt and exhaled the blue-white smoke into his face. "No kidding it was a mistake," she said. "I can see the headlines now: 'Disgruntled Employee at the Hughes Center Enters Premises and Destroys a Quarter-of-a-Million-Dollar Two-Story Window. Details at eleven.'"

"No," Matt said. "I mean I wasn't aiming at the window. I was aiming at this—to get it down so you don't have another attack."

"Attack?" she said.

Grinding splinters of glass noisily shifted and snapped underfoot as Matt approached the gap where the window once stood. He looked up at some pieces pointing toward him. He bent down with his eyes still on the gleaming razor-sharp glass swinging in the breeze, tinkling like lethal wind chimes.

He picked up the black box and handed it to Shepherd. "Show Her Feculence this," he said.

Shepherd shook it and put it to his ear. "What is it?"

"Homing device," Matt said. "I'm going to get the plane."

"Plane," Shepherd said. "What plane? There was no air assault here. There's no way a plane could have been part of an attack here. There would been more Tomcats on the terrorists than you could even imagine, Matt."

"Just give it to her. I'll bring the plane in. It didn't go off, but I guarantee a couple others did."

Dr. Wilhamena Halstead looked at the box Shepherd handed her. She threw it on the floor and watched Matt wade his way through rubble to the garden area. He leaned over the three-foot border surrounding one of the ponds and reached into the water. When he stood up, there was water flowing out of a bent and ragged yellow and blue radio-controlled aircraft. On one wing was a thin cable holding a silver fiberglass canister. It was intact. On the other wing a cable also hung, but with no container.

Matt held the battered aircraft in front of Dr. Halstead.

She sat back down. "What you have there, big guy?" she asked.

"Kind of a poor man's attack drone. A very nice weapon of choice for the terrorist on a budget. You have heard of drones. We use them. The U.S. uses them."

Matt yanked the canister off the left wing.

Dr. Halstead jumped off her chair and slipped on powdered glass to put as much distance between herself and the bomb as possible. The two guards slipped and stumbled trying to keep up to her.

"Here," Matt said calmly. "There's a note. Says 'Happy Anniversary. Hope they got engaged.' Also says, 'This was too easy. You people asleep? Plenty more where this came from.'"

Wilhamena Halstead stood with her guards on either side of her—sentries waiting to attack any target just to prove their worth.

"You know you're fired," she said as she pointed to Matt. "And I want a meeting with you people now."

"I'm fired, Wilhamena. No meeting for me."

The tall security guard from the front gate ran full speed through the front doors, his pistol drawn. There was a buzzing sound behind him, then the vague harmonics of wind and mechanical movement. He stopped and turned, went back out through the metal doors and fired ten shots into the air toward the parking lot.

The radio-controlled drones, the size of model aircraft, came in through the front entrance where the gate guard had entered. The first one, a cute yellow Piper Cub, came in at a few feet above the asphalt parking lot. When it hit the metal and glass of the door, it shattered into pieces around the guard who threw himself onto the ground and buried his face down into a thick pile of carpet.

He saw the second plane coming at him. He turned and ran into the open area of glass Matt had created with Shep's .38mm. The guard stopped and turned, took aim at the small model plane closing in on the entranceway, and threw his gun to the ground. He kept running past The Shark, Matt, Wolfe, Shepherd, and the scattered and frightened secretaries and office workers rummaging through the mess.

When he fell, he instinctively extended his hands in front of him to break the impact. When they hit, he felt pain as glass carved his hands and forearms.

Matt looked down at him and said, "Get up. Can you jump?"

"Sir? What's the matter with you, sir? I'm hurt, bleeding."

"Look at me," Matt said. "Can you jump?"

"Yes, sir. I jumped real well for North Carolina, the Tar Heels, sir, in Chapel Hill, until I blew my knees out my sophomore year. That's why I'm here and living with my mother."

"Then get back to the entrance and pick that other black box off the wall."

"Sir, yes, sir," the guard said.

The box looked as though it belonged there, taking care of some legitimate function at the center.

"Just get it off the wall. Hit it, dunk it, spike it, whatever you can do to get it down here," Matt said. "Then step on it. Nothing will explode."

Sunny grabbed Matt by the arm as security swarmed the plant directing the firefighters and paramedics. "No one is going to listen to you, Matt. No one is going to believe these are radio-controlled model planes and drones having their way with this billion-dollar facility. And what is worse is the fact that whoever is doing it is playing, just toying with us. He could have put more than one of those stupid kid's toys right down our throats with a nuclear device. My intuition tells me that the real thing is next, nuclear or otherwise."

Matt took his arm away from Sunny, stepped back. He looked at her a long time. "Yeah. The real thing is the obvious next step. And we're standing here in the middle of where it will all happen."

Dr. Halstead was enjoying the sound of her raspy voice giving orders to whomever was within earshot. "Dr. Halstead," Matt said. "We have to talk. No time for a meeting. We could have a hundred of those little planes shooting in here with who-knows-what attached to them. Or, if the weather goes down, we're going to have some heavy metal splashing down in the parking lot; I'm talking airliner heavy. Not a pretty scene."

"You're delusional," Dr. Halstead said to Matt. "You have no idea what's going on here. So you found a few homing devices. What's that prove? Nothing. Besides, we don't know yet whether they *are* homing devices."

"You want this to happen, don't you?" Sunny said. "You're not going to do a damn thing to stop it."

Sunny started toward the door. Matt shouted at her. "Where are you going? What can *you* do?"

"Someone has to do something," she said. She went through the open doors. Wolfe followed her.

59

"We have to stop at my condo," Sunny said to Wolfe as they pulled out of the Hughes Center. More trucks and uniformed people came running to the scene as they tried to fight their way through the opposing traffic.

"What, for lunch?" Wolfe said.

"No, for the primitive part we're going to play in this mess. No one else seems to be thinking about how we're being attacked from the air. Tomcats and B-1s can't shoot down radio-controlled model drones. It's so damn simple of a plan and so foolproof. Matt really *is* right for a change. Who can stop the stupid little toys from delivering small explosive devices all day and night? We have to shoot them out of the sky with something until we find the source or locate the attacker. It's a war, by any other name—my God, it's a war."

"And how are we about to do that?" Wolfe said.

"Research, guns, old men with the balls of Watusi Warriors and Big Cheese Helicopter Service. Men who honor the memory of my father. That's how and that's who."

Sunny slid on some sand that had blown across the entrance to the parking lot at the condo. She careened off a large SUV and tore the driver's side door open. A plastic sippy-mug of coffee rolled onto the ground. Wolfe laughed. "Nice, Sunny. Very nice."

Wolfe sat in the car and looked behind him and to the side where Sunny hit the SUV, waiting for the owners to appear. He thought about putting a note on the windshield; then again, maybe not. Sunny turned the corner of the condo at a fast jog. She carried three rifles in her arms as though they were babies. "They were Grampaw's. Dead balls sighted in on target," she said.

"Carry them like that and you're going to have some problems. Know what a 'safety' is?" Wolfe asked.

"No time for safety, Wolfe."

"You thinking to be some sort of contemporary Davy Crockett? Hide and wait for the bad guys in the black hats to announce themselves?"

"No" she said. "Pick them out of the sky one by one until we can get some help. Just bide our time."

"How?" Wolfe asked.

"I'll fly low and slow in the Cirrus. No door on it, anyhow. Do the spotting and call it in to Wink Palmer in the chopper. Wink, an old buddy of Grampaw's, will fly his chopper, Big Cheese, and you'll shoot. I got a few other possibilities for marksmen, too," she said. "I know I am one scared-as-hell English teacher. I love it."

"Those are deer rifles," Wolfe said. "You're not going to hit beans with them."

Wolfe opened his door as Sunny pulled out of the parking slot. His foot hit the pavement before she stopped. He stumbled, regained his balance and jogged over to the trunk of his car. He took out two shotguns, one pump and an over-under. He grabbed boxes of shells and put them into the pockets of his dress pants.

He got back in the car. "I must look like a squirrel with the nuts or shells in the pockets."

"I'm scared to death," Sunny said. "Want to cry and it pisses me off."

"I'm scared, too. Just float with it, like you're in a boat and following where the stream takes you. Just nudge the oar a little to keep you out of trouble. It only takes an inch to miss the jutting rock, not a mile."

"It works for you?" she asked.

"Sometimes."

60

Matt and Shepherd watched Halstead revel in the uniformed attention around her.

"Her Tittilatingness looks good today," Shepherd said.

When they got to Halstead's area, she gestured with her hands for her security and the firemen to leave. They dutifully turned and disappeared into the confusion.

Shepherd stood in front of her and put his hands on his hips, surveyed the damage. "We need sharpshooters stationed all around the perimeter of the plant."

She screwed her face into an expression of disgust. "Sure, like I don't have enough going on here. And what would those stupid fucking sharpshooters be here for anyhow, Shepherd? Tell me—what in the name of all that is technical would they be here for?"

"And they need shotguns. They need a spread, not just a high-powered blast."

"Don't say spread in front of her," Shepherd said.

Halstead looked at Shepherd with the same disgusted contortion of her face. "Oh, you want fired, too?"

Shepherd was silent.

"And the reason for the scatterguns?" Halstead said.

Matt stepped closer to Dr. Halstead. "The reason would be that there are probably more to come. The enemy has nothing to lose but some model-airplane-type drones."

"Oh, I see," Halstead said. "More model planes owned by some seventh-graders accidentally crash into the quad while my staff is picnicking beside the lily pond. You honestly believe we're being attacked by model airplanes?"

Matt raised his hand and pointed to the two areas where the planes had hit. "Those were homing devices and you know it. And the next one could be a lot bigger of an explosion than the first and second. Here's a scrap of fabric that contained a note from the attacker."

Shepherd handed Halstead the yellow, torn piece of fabric from the Cub radio-controlled aircraft. "Says there'll be more to come," he said. "Said Tomcats, radar, nothing will stop them if they want to get through. Also says it doesn't take much to hide at the end of a runway while people are departing for Hawaii and shoot bellies of airliners for kicks and profit."

"It's a ploy," Halstead said. "A distraction. We play model airplane and in addition send out security to watch the approach end of runways all over the country while they do their thing, and we have no idea what it is. Don't you see it?"

Matt grabbed Dr. Halstead by her shoulders and pulled her toward him. There was a smell of mint on her breath and a strong aroma of perfume. He looked at the lines and cracks in the skin under her eyes and the circular outline of contacts. Her shoulder was flesh with little muscle, just the feel of skin and cartilage.

Two large guards started toward them. One reached for his sidearm. The other had his nightstick drawn and extended over his head. Halstead raised her hand as they got to within striking distance. The guards stopped.

She put her hands onto Matt's shoulders and drew him closer. "I am looking at a dead man. What a waste," she said. "What a human waste."

61

Wink, the owner of Big Cheese, had removed the side entry door of the Jet Ranger. Wolfe waved to him and Wink motioned to the back of the chopper. "Throw them in the back," he said.

Wolfe stopped in front of the chopper and carefully looked at each of the shotguns. After he checked the safeties, he put two on the floor of the Ranger. He ran over to where Sunny was stepping up onto the wing of the Cirrus. He handed her the last shotgun. "Put it in the back," he said.

Two men walked toward the Cirrus. They were in their mid to late seventies. Both walked with a limp. One wore a blue denim jacket and jeans. The other had on white Dockers and a red Izod sweater. They were at top speed, walking very slowly. Both wore baseball caps, low over their eyes and sunglasses too big for their shrinking and aged faces.

"Poor Man, Spiffy," Sunny shouted.

Neither heard her. They kept walking.

She raised her voice. "Over there," she said. "Wink's chopper. The guns are there, like I told you guys. You in the chopper, me and Wolfe in the Cirrus."

They still didn't hear her. When they got to the Cirrus, Sunny got out of the cockpit and stood up on the wing. "Didn't wear your hearing aids, did you?"

"Things are a pain in the ass," the man in the Izod said.

"Have Wink shut down and maybe we can all hear ourselves think," the man in the denim said. "We need to talk some more, Sunny. Need a bit more information than your ten-second phone call. We'll do anything for you, but you know what your pappy always said about plans and time and communication. We have to talk. Can't just tell me what to shoot. I may be dumb but I'm not stupid."

Sunny motioned to Wink and the whining sound of blades cutting into air shifted to a slightly lower pitch as he cut the power. The door of the Jet Ranger opened and Wink stepped onto the pavement.

He was obviously older than the two friends who had forgotten their hearing aids. He wore cargo pants, a matching long-sleeved khaki shirt with large breast pockets and a safari vest. Before he turned to start toward the Cirrus, he reached back into the helicopter and grabbed an Aussie Outback hat, put it on his head and measured the distance between brim and eyebrow with his middle and index finger. He didn't have a limp.

The three old men, Wolfe and Sunny stood in a circle between the nose and left wing of the plane. The one in the denim went up to Sunny and put his arms out. She moved toward him and put her arms around him. The other two went over and joined in the group hug.

No aircraft were flying. It was quiet except for the sound of wind gusts moving through the metal fencing surrounding the airport. There was the occasional yelp of a seagull.

Wolfe broke the silence. "What am I, chopped liver?" he said. The old men laughed as Sunny stepped away from the group. She dabbed her forehead with a handkerchief, then wiped some tears from her eyes.

There was the bustling and rustling of feet on the cement as the men jockeyed for position to shake Wolfe's hand. There was also the sound of attempted formal introductions that were made too fast to mean anything. But the faces, the ages, the loyalty to a lady and her grandfather meant something the proper introductions could not replace, a chemistry of the soul.

Sunny blew her nose and said it first. "We're going to shoot radio-controlled planes, lethal drones, out of the sky at the Hughes Center. We're going to go in on a practice instrument approach at Atlantic City International and look for riflemen at the approach and departure ends of the runway."

Wink took his silly hat off. "Then what, Sunny? What do we do to top that for one day's fun?"

"I don't know, Wink. I don't know. We shoot the planes out of the sky. If we see someone on their back with a high power rifle at ACY waiting to take shots at aircraft, we'll see. You tell me. You guys fought a couple wars. I teach English and fly planes. Those things used to be fun. Now, there isn't any left, I don't think."

62

Trog Svladen walked into the entrance of the Hughes Technical Center like he was walking onto a stage and he was the best player, the only player, the one player left because all the others had been killed. He felt calmness in his armor of disguise and secure in the becoming of something he was not. In this case, it was a man in navy blue work pants and shirt. He had a white cotton patch over his left breast pocket had the inscriptions in red letters: "GLASS ETCHING BY WILLIE."

"And you are?" the security guard at the front entrance of the facility asked.

"Willie, obviously, young man."

"You're not on the list, not emergency, medical, or firefighter services."

"I was called a month ago to etch some glass doors to offices. I am here. I can't help if you people can't keep this place together without things blowing up. My work is in the basement, anyhow. Probably not much going on down there. Is there?"

"Can't discuss that with you, sir," the uptight, upright, guard said to the glass etcher.

"My ass is itchy," the etcher said. "And I don't feel good. What kind of atmospheric crap did you people get here, anyhow? I feel dizzy. I think—I think I'm going to fall."

Trog started to tilt backward toward some oncoming cars and trucks that were heading into the activity at the center. There was the screech of tires on hot pavement, sirens, the blowing of horns.

The guard helped the etcher into the guardhouse. He moved slowly and spread his legs carefully when he took a step. Trog sat down and gagged. He leaned over so as to avoid messing up his perfectly-pressed navy work clothes and produced nothing but a dry-heave of saliva and noise.

Trog tore the front of his shirt and put his right hand on the center of his chest. "Maybe my heart," he said. "Maybe get too old for this. Retire."

The guard was obviously disturbed by the man's suffering.

Trog looked him silently in the eyes for a long time as he gasped for air. "You know CPR, young man?"

"I'll call medical," he said. "Just one minute."

The guard reached up to the microphone attached squarely to the epaulet on his right shoulder. He crooked his neck and tilted his head and spoke into the mike. As he did, Trog stood slowly with his right hand gently supporting his crotch area.

"What are you doing, buddy," the guard said, "playing with yourself?

He stood up and took a large swallow of air. The guard's hand was still on the talk button of the microphone on his shoulder. Trog forced his hand away from his crotch, took the thin aviation safety wire from his breast pocket and pulled out the safety-wiring device from his hip pocket. "Twist and shout," he said to the guard.

The guard looked at the man now standing strongly in front of him with no bent shoulders, no sobs, grunts, groans, or hacking coming from his chest.

He put the thin cutting wire around the guard's neck. The guard's expression changed as he attempted to put his hand between the cutting wire and the spinning pliers. His middle and index fingers slammed against his neck as Trog pulled the twist mechanism on the tool and the wire constricted through the fingers and halfway through the man's neck before it stopped abruptly on bone.

Trog stepped back and looked at the two fingers on the floor. He kicked them under a table holding some steaming coffee and a sandwich in aluminum foil. He lifted up the sandwich and took a bite. A red splotch appeared on the genital area his hand had been supporting. He chewed slowly so as not to disturb the stitches in his mouth.

The etcher lifted the guard onto the desk and tilted the upper torso of the body at a forty-five degree level in order to keep the blood flowing away from the guard's uniform. He unbuttoned the jacket, took it off the guard and patted his hand onto some of the blood that was running onto the floor. He wiped it onto his face. "Matches the bloody uniform nicely," he mumbled.

He stripped off the pants, put them over his pants, pulled the belt tight and took a roll of Velcro out of his pocket. He bent over, stuck it to the inside of the long pants he'd just taken off the guard and folded them to a neat cuff that rested and broke to a crease on his shoe.

Outside, cars and trucks went in and out of the facility. Trog periodically stuck his head up to the window, smiled and waved to the passing emergency vehicles.

He got down onto the floor, pushed his hands against the thin wall of the guard station and shoved the limp body under the table. He draped his shirt over the body. He took a computer monitor off the table, dropped it to the floor and slid it to cover the rest of the body.

He stepped toward the open door of the guardhouse, stopped, turned around and took an M16 out of a corner. He threw the weapon and strap over his right shoulder, looked to see that his handgun was secure on his hip, and slapped his left calf to feel the slim hard body of the knife.

"How you say in American?" he said to himself. "It showtime?"

63

"How many of us are dying a day?" Spiffy said.

"What do you mean, 'how many'?" Poor Man asked.

"I mean veterans."

Poor Man slapped Spiffy on the back and said, "Too damn many. That's how many. Virtually every WWII veteran is over 70. We're a bit old, but we are loyal to what is right."

Wolfe moved in close to the group of old men who were talking like it was a Saturday morning donut and coffee clutch. "Please," he said, "with all due respect, and I do mean that sincerely, we have to get on the job here. Terrorists don't wait and don't have a great deal of..."

Wink straightened his hat and laughed. "They were just trying to get through the day like the rest of us," he said. "All of a sudden they were getting medals pinned on them. And, by the way, young man, you go off and do something *fast* with no plan in a situation like this, you'll be doing something wrong. Besides, tack a few decades to your years and a few major surgeries and handicaps and see how fast you are."

Wolfe put his hand to his mouth and coughed. "Sorry," he said.

"So let me get this right," Wink said looking at Sunny. "You believe someone on the inside is getting homing devices planted at the Hughes facility to wreck the place. But on the other hand, you think it may be a diversion because there are going to be some yo-yos lying on their backs with high-power rifles blasting holes in airliners as they depart Atlantic City International Airport."

Sunny said, "Yes."

"And, the plan is," Wink continued slowly, "you fly the Cirrus low and slow, spot the RCs coming into the center. You call it in to us, we pick them out of the sky one by one, then when we feel all warm and cuddly that all that mess is cleared up, we head for ACY and shoot whoever is lying on their backs on the departure or approach ends of the runway. Well, you young folks, sounds like a plan to me."

Wink, Sunny and Wolfe turned simultaneously and looked at Spiffy and Poor Man. "Well?" Sunny said.

"Now I don't mind," Spiffy said, "that I could be shot out of the sky today by a pilot in a Tomcat with a big expensive watch and a big young man's dick. I really don't. It would be a good day if I was doing the right thing. But for the sake of discussion, what about getting shot out of the sky?"

Poor Man turned and walked to his car, opened the trunk and pulled out a tattered Ninth Air Force flag and an enormous American Flag. "These both go on the ship I fly and maybe die in, or I don't take this trip," he said. "I die with these and it will have been a good day. And I don't mean just take them. I mean, fly the colors."

Wink took the flags over to Big Cheese. "It'll take a few minutes, that's all," he shouted back at the group. "Now, someone's going to have to hold them inside until I get to altitude, otherwise they'll touch the ground. And by the way, I have no safeties in the back of the chopper. Don't lean out too far if you shoot. The first step is a *real* bitch."

"Not a problem," Spiffy said.

64

Captain Jack "Jocko" Shotson, age twenty-nine, settled into the ejection seat of the F-14 Tomcat at Dover Air Force Base in Dover, Delaware. He dialed in Dover Tower on 126.35 and waited for incoming traffic to clear visual sequencing 25 miles out.

He punched in Automatic Terminal Information Service and listened to weather: WNW, 300 degrees, wind at 30 knots, gusting to 48, visibility ten miles.

He looked down at the clipboard on his right knee, noted wind direction for his return to Dover and circled the 48 KT wind speed thinking that even in a strike and reconnaissance aircraft like the Tomcat, 50+ mile-per-hour winds were a factor.

He reached down and pulled his orders out of the pocket on his left calf. Standard recon at the Hughes Research and Development Center; no more than a minute or two away from his location.

He knew there would be some Coast Guard choppers below him and had their frequencies on his clipboard. The orders said nothing about radio-controlled aircraft, nothing about homing devices at the Center, nothing about suspected terrorist activity, nothing about rifles at Atlantic City.

He felt the kick as he applied power for his departure from Dover. He carried only basic armament for the patrol mission: the General Electric Vulcan M61A-1 20mm gun with 675 rounds of ammunition, Rockeye bomb and cluster bombs and one medium-range Sidewinder air to air missile.

Captain Shotson banked the Tomcat steeply to intercept his on course heading. He felt the G-forces and welcomed them. He thought he was going to have another boring patrol day with nothing to do but watch.

65

"Over 50 mile-per-hour gusts," Sunny said to Wolfe as she stepped up onto the wing of the Cirrus. "Buckle up tight when you get in there. I can imagine the headlines," she said. "Retired Special Agent Rendered Unconscious While Flying in Restricted Airspace. Pilot Held for Questioning."

Wolfe put his headset on and gave a sarcastic laugh. "Very funny, Sunny. You may not be too far off if this doesn't go right. That airspace is out of bounds for us. How you going to handle that?"

Poor Man walked up to the front of Sunny's Cirrus and waved at her. He was holding a hat in his right hand. He held it up and pointed to it.

"What?" Sunny said. "We're losing time now, Poor. We have to get going. This front is moving in and I'm looking at some serious black clouds over there."

"Now, girl," Poor Man said with a creamy kindness and calmness in his voice. "You wear this hat. It's your grandfather's fifty-mission hat from the war." He handed it to Sunny. "Call me sentimental," he said. "Just wear it."

"It smells," she said.

"Mothballs will do that," Poor Man shouted over the gusting winds. "I know how silly it is of me to ask you this. Humor me. Put it on and don't take it off until you land safely here at the end of the day."

Sunny shouted back at Poor Man. He put his hands to both of his ears. "Can't hear you," he said. "Just wear it."

Poor Man turned and walked as briskly as he could to the chopper. He looked up to see Wink snapping the brim of his Aussie hat.

Poor Man sat down on the floor of the chopper, lifted one leg up then the other. He rolled over on all fours, stood up, took the one step to where Spiffy was sitting and grabbed the headset hanging from a hook and put it on. "Hey Wink, Spiffy—kick the tire and light the fire. Let's go kick some enemy ass if we can tell the good guys from the bad ones."

The chopper rose only inches off the taxiway at Cape May County when a 50-mile-per-hour gust slapped it down onto the right skid. Instead of forcing it up, Wink gently reduced power and let it settle down again.

"Let's try that again," he said. "Fly no chopper before its time. Baby just wasn't ready."

Just over the runway threshold, Wink looked back at the two old friends sitting beside each other, shotguns between their legs and flags held gently in their hands, ragged VFW baseball hats with post number and their names. He nodded toward the open door and Poor Man and Spiffy unfurled the flags over the side.

"Been a good day so far, gentlemen," Wink said.

He glanced back again, waiting for a response to come over the intercom. The two men held their weapons at eye level, pumped and ejected some shells and picked them up. They reloaded and then calmly looked down at the ocean beneath them on the way to the Hughes Center.

Wink followed the beach, the men looking down at sunbathers wondering whether or not to chance the impending storm. As the three looked over the side of the Big Cheese, they couldn't understand why so many sunbathers were standing up.

"What the hell is going on?" Spiffy said. "They're standing up."

"The flag," Wink said.

"Fuckin'A," Poor Man added.

"When's the last time you guys fired a scatter gun?" Wink asked.

"Nineteen fifty-one or '52 for me," Poor Man said.

Spiffy scratched his chin and thought. "I think the eighties or nineties for me. Like riding a bicycle, though."

There was the sound of static over the intercom from the approaching storm and the periodic request from approach control demanding the two unidentified aircraft to identify themselves.

"Didn't know you were all that current and well practiced, guys."

Spiffy tapped Wink on the shoulder with the shotgun. "Who would those unidentified aircraft be?" he said.

There was a silence.

"That be us with Sunny," he said. "We're not allowed to be here, at least today we're not."

66

Captain Shotson heard the southern twang of his radar intercept officer in the backseat of the Tomcat break the radio silence. "Well, Jock, I don't know why those Coast Guard types aren't calling us up here. I see two targets below us. One appears to be a chopper and the other a quick little private plane. At least that'd be my guess. I got the Coast Guarders identified, but those other two little guys are targets, at least by my definition. Aye, Jock? What say you, man? We allowed to waste them?"

Captain Shotson chuckled into the intercom. "You trigger-happy teenagers crack me up," he said. "Paint one unidentified picture on a radar screen and you want to hit the pickle button and make smoke. How old are you?"

The back seat rider, Lieutenant Charles T. (Spider Bite) Amerson, laughed.

"Anyhow, let's take a look," Shotson said. He poked in the Coast Guard frequency. "Coast Guard 9. Big Green here."

A female voice replied from the Coast Guard chopper, "Go ahead, Green."

"Got two boogies you guys are missing. Think we're going to come on down and take a look."

"Just about to call you," the Coast Guard helicopter replied. "Not sure their intentions. They're not answering any of our calls. We're thinking maybe they're lost."

On the Tomcat intercom Spider Bite said, "I love the sound of female voices over military radios. Jock, do you get a picture of her when she talks? I mean a picture in your head?"

"Settle down, big boy. Here we go."

Shotson inverted the Tomcat, pulled back on the stick and felt the G-forces pressing. He felt his heart pound and welcomed the adrenalin release into his system.

On the intercom he heard the RIO say, "I just love when you play rough. Okay, I'm sorry, boss. I'm settled down now. All business. Jock, it's getting really dark with this front moving in. Would be great to use the Catseye Night-Vision stuff in the middle of the day."

Shotson didn't reply. There was just the crackle of radio static and breathing.

In the distance, somewhere out over the Atlantic, a flash of lightning lit up the eastern sky. Somewhere there was the roll of thunder. Over the Hughes Center, there was the sound of helicopters, a private plane, and the unmistakable roar of two General Electric F110-GE-400 turbofan engines slowing down, throttling back to slow fly and identify the intruders.

"Hey, Jock," the RIO said. "I'm just killing time here. I'm sure this is just another walk in the park."

"Maybe, Spider. We'll see."

67

Sunny saw a flash of color, pulled back the throttle and raised the nose of the Cirrus to reduce airspeed. She pushed heavy left rudder to get a look at the camo-colored radio-controlled plane heading for the Center.

"Hey guys," she said into the boom mike. "This one isn't bright. This one is camo. What's that tell you?" There was silence and then Sunny's voice. "Do it, Mikey. Do it."

"Sunny, I'll only ask once. Are you sure?"

Sunny looked over at Wolfe. He put the bird-spotting binoculars on his lap and shook his head.

Sunny pushed the talk switch. "Do it," she said.

In the darkening sky, a bright splash of ballistic display lightened up the Hughes Center plant like one of the approaching storm cells. In the back seat of Big Cheese, Spiffy was bent over picking up five spent shotgun shells off the Jet Ranger floor. "One for five isn't bad," he said. "Not at my age."

68

"Not a cake walk," the RIO said to Captain Shotson. "That was a formidable blast. What was it?"

"Not a clue," Shotson said. "Let's see."

He pulled back the throttles and the variable sweep wings of the Tomcat moved forward to assist his slow flight to keep speed down to just above stalling. He nudged in beside the helicopter target.

Both naval aviators looked into the open doors of the Jet Ranger. The flipped up the dark UV sunscreens on their flight helmets. They unsnapped their oxygen masks. Captain Shotson grabbed his ox mask and pushed it close enough for the intercom to pick up his voice. "You hear me, Spider?"

"Yepper, boss."

"Do you see what I see? Tell me what you see."

"Jock, forgive me, but I see three old men, one in an Aussie hat and photography vest, two in the back seat trying for the Arnie Palmer look and packing a couple squirrel guns."

"You are correct, my friend. So do I."

"Take me to the white thing over there," Spider said. "Over there to that little plane. Check it out. No door."

Gingerly and with great care not to stall the 43,000-pound aircraft, Captain Shotson eased in beside Sunny's Cirrus. Spider looked closely as the jet slid in on Sunny's left side. Shotson looked in at Sunny, her hair blowing underneath the fifty-mission hat. He looked over at Wolfe with the bird-watching binoculars gazing out of the other side of the aircraft.

Wolfe glanced at the Tomcat at their nine o'clock position and went back to the binoculars, scouring the grounds surrounding the Hughes Center. He tapped Sunny on the shoulder.

She flicked his hand away. “Please, not now,” she said. “I’m dealing with a couple young officers beside us here. And they’re in one kick-ass killing machine.”

“Make friends with them,” Wolfe said. “Better yet, tell them there are at least a half dozen radio-controlled planes, probably no bigger than their helmets, below them somewhere. We’ve shot down a couple with the scatterguns. Tell them they can’t use their firepower to get these things. Obviously they’d take out the entire plant when their rockets impacted the ground. We’re the only game in town, Sunny. You got to do this sale job. Turn it on. Show some leg or something. These guys are young and impressionable.”

“Very funny, Wolfe. Very.”

Sunny dialed in the 121.5 emergency frequency on her radio. As soon as the LED screen illuminated, she heard Captain Shotson’s voice. “Cirrus over the Hughes Center. Follow me.”

Sunny looked over at the face of Captain Shotson. It was obvious that he had his hands full keeping the Tomcat at the slower Cirrus speed. It was the serious face of a young man with a mission. She looked in the back at the weapons system officer. He smiled broadly, took the Nomex glove off his left hand and waved.

In the cockpit of the Tomcat, the RIO said to Shotson, “This cracks me up, Jocko. It really does. Look at that lady. What’s going on here? We can’t shoot her. Maybe pellets. Give me a pellet gun. That’s it.”

Shotson ignored the comments as he struggled with the controls, marginal speed, and increasing gusts from the approaching cold front.

“My God, Sunny,” Wolfe pleaded. “Can’t you slow this thing down? Maybe hit these gusts a little slower so they don’t beat us up so much? Wow. We’re going to be black and blue.”

Sunny shrugged her shoulders. “You better hope that’s all we’ll be. If we are, just consider yourself lucky. Damn it, Wolfe, you talk. I can’t slow this down. If I do, I’ll lose the Tomcat because they won’t be able to match my slow flight. They’ll think we’re running by actually going slower. Who knows what they’ll do?”

Wolfe keyed the mike. “Tomcat, Cirrus here. Gentlemen, I am an FBI retiree assisting on a case with a Hughes Center employee. The plant has been hit with some explosions that we have reason to believe were delivered by radio-controlled aircraft. We have shot down two with scatterguns from the Jet Ranger. There are at least six more we have spotted. Hard to tell, though. They are all Piper Cub models so the count may be wrong.”

Sunny looked at the smile on the face of the RIO fade.

Immediately over the radio Sunny and Wolfe heard the voice of Shotson. "Stand by, Cirrus."

Sunny watched the orange glow of afterburners ignite in the back of the Tomcat. "I'd say they're going to climb into some calmer air, relax a minute and call their air boss for instructions. What do you suppose they'll be told to do?"

Wolfe looked at her, smiled slightly and said, "I don't want to think about it."

69

Big Cheese broke in on the emergency frequency. "Sunny, go to air-to-air frequency."

Sunny dialed in the air-to-air. "Go ahead, Wink. How you guys holding up?"

"Not a problem here, Sunny. Ah, we listened in on the emergency frequency to the discussion with your new friends in the jet with the afterburners and big guns. Maybe put in a good word for us because we are the ones with the shotguns. They might frown upon that if they don't decide we're friends."

Big Cheese and the Cirrus were flying below their recommended cruise speeds to lighten the blows made by the turbulence.

"Nice spring rain that started here today, aye Sunny?" Wink said.

"Yeah. It's blowing in pretty good now. And that's no spring rain, Wink. It's serious black-cloud rain. Let's change headings; maybe keep it hitting the unexposed sides. I'm really taking on water with the door gone."

They turned 90 degrees to the right. "There, that's better," Sunny said.

She gave Wink a thumbs up. She looked into the back of the chopper where Poor Man and Spiffy held their weapons on their laps as they stuck their heads outside looking for deadly little yellow radio-controlled Piper Cubs with explosive charges attached to their wings. Spiffy was soaked from the downpour. Sunny saw him take his shirt off, reach in a duffle bag and take out a white T-shirt and two navy blue baseball hats. He put it on and pulled the brim down over his eyes. He opened a leather case, took out a pair of yellow shooting glasses and put them on. He handed a cap to Poor Man, who folded the brim to the correct bend and put it on.

Wink looked back at them, both with too many gold chains around their necks, too much sun, hair too bleached and too much smell of gunpowder for their own good. "You guys look like you're heading for a whore house, not a terrorist shooting stand-off," Wink said. "Well, except for the VFW hats. They make the outfit."

Spiffy saluted Wink, took his weapon off his lap and said, "Let's get this over with, whether those boys with the big dicks and guns come back or not. Fuck it. Let's go. Whatever happens, whatever goes down, it will have been a good day."

"Bye," Wink said as he waved to Sunny and pointed the nose of the chopper directly at the Hughes Complex. "You heard the man, Sunny. We'll be down there a few feet off the deck, looking up. When we see yellow, we're taking the Cubs out, Tomcat or no Tomcat. Is that affirmed?" he said.

Sunny keyed her mike twice. Wink keyed his as Big Cheese took position directly over the main building.

"Sunny," Wink said. "I'm going to have to either land on the roof or hover higher. Otherwise this wind is going to take all of our problems away in one big splash."

"Cirrus and Ranger at the Hughes Center," Captain Shotson's voice said over the radio. "Stand by. Listen up. And listen up real good."

70

The Shark stood her ground in front of Matt and Shepherd, arms on hips, head high and jaw set. "You both are wrong. There is no attack. There was an accident and you are overreacting in the face of panic. I can't believe you don't have your collective acts together in a no-brain situation like this. There's even a fighter of some kind assigned to us. What more could you want? A couple Coast Guard choppers from the base in Wildwood, too?"

Through the gaping window that had been blasted, there was the incoming sound of engines—the Tomcat, helicopters and sirens still arriving at the Center. In the background over the Atlantic, lightning lit the blackening day and the sound of thunder snapped heads to the sky as they wondered if it was Mother Nature or just another accident.

"Put the cuffs on him, Shepherd. Put the cuffs on Matt and get him out of here," Dr. Halstead said. "It frightens me to think what he might do in his present state."

"Present state?" Matt asked. "What are you talking about? You're the one who is choked and crazy, making lame decisions, lady."

"Put them on, Shepherd."

Shepherd reached under his blazer and took out the handcuffs. He took Matt's arms, pinned the wrists behind his back and snapped the cuffs around them. There was the sharp snap of a metal lock.

Shepherd grabbed Matt's forearm and escorted him through the front door and into the pouring rain. They stopped, looked up at Big Cheese above the roof and the crew of three inside. In the distance they saw the Cirrus and fighter flying as though in formation, but they knew these weren't weekend pilots out for a joy ride on their way for lunch.

Shepherd released Matt's arm, reached into his breast pocket and took out a key and unlocked the cuffs. "This is getting real basic," he said, "real simple. I like that. Get to the Wreck, take the shotgun out of the trunk, get in the car and wait. Oh, Matt, here's your fanny pack. Got any lunch in there?"

Matt put the black and yellow pack around his waist and headed for the Rent-A-Wreck. He stuck the key into the trunk lock and turned. Nothing happened. He hit the top of the trunk with his fist. It popped open. He reached in and took out a twelve-gauge pump shotgun, looked around like some sort of criminal, realizing he was starting to feel like one, and got into the car. He drove to the center of the parking lot, wedged himself between a Lincoln Navigator and a red Toyota Sequoia, essentially rendering the old car invisible.

He got out, and gently as he could, with the butt of the gun, smashed the windshield, side windows and finally the rear window. He tapped the jagged glass remaining around the windows.

He got back into the Wreck and mumbled, "A wreck by any other name." He felt his hand slipping on the gun, as it became difficult to hold. He looked at his Dockers and the dirty beige seat to his right and saw blood. He put the gun down and looked at his palms dripping onto the shirt, seat, and the stupid fanny pack. He took a piece of tape out of the pack, turned the key and taped the windshield wiper washers "on." He again got out of the car and placed his bleeding hands into the soap and alcohol flow of the washer fluid. He screamed at the pain and kept holding them in the flow. The green liquid mixed with the blood and flowed onto the dash and instruments in the car. He stayed until the washers were empty and made the exhausted pumping and sucking noise of compressors with nothing to compress.

The amount of blood soaking into the dash of the car surprised him. He felt dizzy, not knowing if it was from the loss of blood or just the sight of the stuff dripping down the speedometer and the rest of the instruments, creating the illusion of an accident—bodies and ambulances arriving to save lives.

He thought about looking for something to wrap his hands with but realized it would hinder his shooting. There wouldn't be time to unwrap them and feel the gun and weight and instinct he needed to lead the target and pull the trigger. He sat in the passenger's seat in the full recline position. He leaned up and turned the key on again and pushed the sunroof button. Nothing happened.

He got out and checked the safety of the shotgun, grabbed it by the barrel as though the weapon were a sledgehammer and banged repeatedly on the glass of the roof until it broke into pieces and fell onto the front seats. He brushed some large chunks of glass out of the back seat with the butt of the gun. He felt the barrel slip in his wet, bloody hands.

The storm had entered the violent phase. There was the loud, pelting downpour with periodic splats of ice pellets hitting the pavement and either smashing into nothingness or bouncing a foot into the air.

Matt thought about Sunny and Wolfe in the Cirrus; Wink, Spiffy and Poor Man in Big Cheese. He stood up on the rear seat and looked through the opening he had made in the roof. Wink had landed the Jet Ranger on the roof of the Hughes Center. All three of them were standing on the skids adding their collective weight to keep it from blowing away.

He looked around for the Coast Guard choppers and saw nothing. He realized they had apparently been ordered off the scene when the full blast of the storm hit. He saw the Cirrus buffeting up then down and finally disappearing into the low black clouds over the ocean. He kept standing, looking, waiting for it to reappear or for the weather to show some small sign of letting up. There was no Cirrus, Sunny or Wolfe.

The dark part of his mind imagined them sitting in a soaking wet cabin with radios sparking and failing in the moisture. He saw the open door, the binoculars that had been used for happier days spotting finches and rare birds returning from South America and taking a break in the marshes of Cape May. He looked down and saw the blood on his hands and felt his head become heavy, realizing it wasn't the thought of an accident that was making him dizzy.

He waited for a target of opportunity, sitting in the seat soaked with his blood and the fresh, cool rain from the sea.

He looked up through the roof of the Wreck and in his confusion chuckled at the name "Wreck" and wondered what the agency would say when he returned it. Maybe there would be congratulations in order, maybe some sort of design award, maybe a new and improved wreck citation of honor for all the broken glass and bloodstained seats.

He pushed the windshield wipers on and watched them struggle in their mechanical chaos as they bumped and tore into the dash. More wreck awards at the return.

He looked up again into the empty storm of the sky and saw only the Tomcat and the sudden ignition of the afterburners just below the black layer of clouds. He knew they would be returning to Dover and waiting out the most severe part of the storm. He also knew there was no sign of Sunny since the winds had sucked the Cirrus into the darkness.

He leaned his head back on the headrest. He closed his eyes and felt the nausea in his stomach and the burn of pain on his hands. He heard the patter of rain on the hood, the tick-tock banging of the useless wipers and the pounding of his heart.

71

In the wet darkness of the Cirrus, Sunny fought the controls to keep the aircraft upright.

Wolfe tightened his harness and shouted over the wind rushing in through where the door had been. "Why not turn on the autopilot? Why hand-fly it, Sunny? The autopilot will keep the blue side up, as they say. I know there is no blue side now, but you know what I mean. Hell, we might be inverted or in a spin. Please, turn it on. You have a sick bag for me, Sunny? I'm going to be real sick now."

Sunny ignored him as she looked over to see him put his head toward the floor and stay there for a long time.

"Nothing works, Wolfe. We have a foot of water on the floor and who knows what behind the panel. We're lucky nothing has ignited."

"What's that noise?" Wolfe said as he wiped his mouth with his forearm. "That loud pounding."

"Hail," Sunny said.

"Where are we?" Wolfe said.

"I have no idea, Wolfe Man, but we are climbing like hell and I'm pushing down, not up, on the yoke. We should be descending, but the thermals are unreal here, taking us up."

"I can't breathe," he said.

"We're at 30,000 feet with no oxygen. I didn't bring it, thought we'd be nowhere near an altitude where we'd need oxygen."

"Fishing, that's what to do," Wolfe said. "Little worm fish, that's what. I fished with my brother on the Allegheny and ate the fish, too. Let us fish, by God."

"Hypoxia," Sunny said. "We're getting hypoxia from the lack of pressure at this altitude. Brain starving for it, making no sense for it, not sense, fishing. Oh, shit. Passing out."

In the distance, through the swirling winds and powerful thermals, Sunny saw a thin slice of yellow, a light that was either in her mind or in her flight path. She couldn't be sure.

She pulled the throttle back, reached over to Wolfe and snugged his harness until she could not force it any tighter. She reached down to hers and did the same as she shouted over the noise of wind and idling engine, "Fishing worms, I smell," and her eyes closed.

72

Matt's eyes opened to see the last splashes of rain hit the hood. It felt like the end of a bad dream, the part where the sun comes out and everyone waves hello or goodbye and lovers embrace and music plays.

He glanced to the east and watched the trailing edge of the storm disperse out to sea, and behind it the bright rays of a cleansed sky. He stretched a warm, featherbed stretch in the front seat of the Rent-A-Wreck, forgetting his slashed hands until he instinctively flexed them.

He rubbed his eyes and felt the moisture again and all the memories came back: the loss of blood, the nausea, and the wild storm. He reached into the fanny pack, pulled out a roll of surgical gauze and wrapped both hands, leaving only the index finger and thumb exposed. He remembered reading a book that said how ancient warriors would cut off the thumbs of their enemies when captured, thus rendering them unable to throw a spear or wield a sword. He chuckled and looked down at the soggy fanny pack on his lap and said into the clear air, "Or fly a Tomcat?"

He reached beside him on the seat and picked up the shotgun. He knew with the violent updrafts and downdrafts in the storm there would be no radio-controlled Cubs flying in to blow anything up. The calm, however, after the storm was another matter. The time was now and he knew if it was going to happen, if the ridiculous little yellow planes were going to attack the center, it would be now.

He looked straight up into the blue sky, stuck his right index finger in front of his face and pulled an imaginary trigger. "Bang, bang," he whispered as he watched a flag unfurl above his position, the flag still attached to the bottom of Wink's chopper.

The chopper stopped in mid-air, directly at his 12 o'clock position. There was a bang from the port then the starboard sides. Matt stood up on his seat, stuck his torso out the sunroof of the Toyota and saw pieces of yellow sprinkle onto the parking lot.

The chopper moved slowly, making a 360-degree arc as it eased toward the main building of the Hughes Center.

Matt settled down into his prone position again, shotgun on his chest, his finger on the trigger, his eyes looking into the empty sky, waiting.

73

In the storm that Matt had seen disappear into the east, Sunny and Wolfe sat cold and shivering. Wolfe opened his eyes wide. "Water is falling to the ceiling," he shouted to Sunny. "It is. I am not under the influence of hypoxia. I know up from down. I think."

Sunny pointed to his headset as she put hers back on. "We're only at five thousand feet, Wolfe. Oxygen not a problem now. You're right. I don't know how we got here but the ambient temp is warmer, no turbulence, just cloud. It is falling up. Why? Oh shit, Wolfe, we're inverted. The water on the floor, all that accumulation from the open door, it's falling up because we're upside down."

Sunny heard the engine of the Cirrus sputter for the first time. "This plane is one hell of a machine, Wolfe. I can't believe the beating it has taken and it's still flying. Airliners wouldn't be willing to fly through what we've gone through. But the water from the inside, everything. I don't know how it can keep going."

There was the swish of winged silence as the last of the up-flowing water dissipated from the roof of the plane. Sunny talked to herself as the G-forces pressed her into the seat. "We're inverted, Grampaw. We have to be. Water is flowing up. So, pull back on the yoke instead of pushing forward to point the nose down."

Sunny looked at Wolfe, his eyes closed and hands braced against the instrument panel, anticipating impact.

"Open them, Wolfe," Sunny said. "You'll get more vertigo than you already have. Sicker. Don't close them now."

"What the hell is up or down anyhow?" he asked. "It's starting not to matter."

74

"Guys, we're getting low on fuel," Wink said. "Not much more we can do here, especially if we're going to be sucking fumes."

"Take me to the Cement Ship," Spiffy said. "I have my flag ceremony to do. Every night one of us does it. Kids come in, scouts or a class from school and they help. Hey, what a grandstand entrance in Big Cheese. Right, guys?"

"Not a problem if I take on some fuel once we're there," he said. "I'll just follow the coast up to the ceremony area. Ya know, it's getting late, Spiffy. You better tell them you'll be there."

"Take me there. Perfect ending to a great day," he said.

Wink throttled back to conserve fuel as he slowly cruised up the Atlantic coastline. They looked down at the diehard beach-goers lazily dragging their towels and blankets back onto the sand after the storm. Poor Man leaned out the side of the chopper and tugged on the ropes that were holding the flag secure. "I'll reel it in just before we land. You have enough fuel, Wink, to do one low pass before you go in?"

"I'll make enough fuel," he said.

The Cement Ship was an experiment during the war that went afoul off the tip of New Jersey. The remains of it were still visible from the tourist area at the very tip of the Jersey Shore. The ship had become more than a tourist attraction over the years. It had become a badge of pride and honor where, during the tourist season, the American flag was unfurled at sunset by a veteran and usually a student, Cub Scout or other youth from the community. There were often tears during the playing of taps and the tears were from old and young alike. For Wink, Poor Man and Spiffy, there was no doubt in their minds they would be trying to keep their composure during this particular ceremony.

Wink looked at his fuel gauge and crossed his fingers as he saw the wrecked ship, flag and buildings come into view. Purely for the sake of drama and a grand entrance, he lowered the nose, pointed it at the flag and bulk of the tourists who were looking up at him. From a position about a half-mile out to sea, he started his high-speed approach.

Behind Wink, the pilot and RIO of an F-14 Tomcat set up on a strategic track. It pointed directly at the speeding chopper as it headed for the crowd of onlookers.

Poor Man and Spiffy stood up and braced themselves beside the open door of the chopper. They both bent down and grabbed either part of the flag flowing below the helicopter, ready to reel it in before the chopper touched down on the sand.

Spiffy looked back to see the sunset before they landed. He shouted to Poor Man and Wink. "Beautiful," he said. "Look at that sunset. Look at it sparkle."

Poor Man turned to see the sparkle. It wasn't the sun.

The explosion was at a safe distance from the crowd as they watched Big Cheese disintegrate in the beautiful ocean sunset. The debris fell only a hundred yards away from the sunken ship. The flag they were reeling in floated gently on the easy evening waves of the Atlantic.

"Got them just in time," the RIO said to the front seat Tomcat driver. "There were kids and parents, grammaws and grampaws down there. The bastards."

The crowd stood in silence as the Tomcat turned toward Dover. A veteran walked over to the flagpole, cleared his throat and looked at the young boy standing at attention beside the flag, still gently cracking in the wind. The old man motioned to the bugler to start the traditional taps.

The man cleared his throat, shook the boy's hand and said in a tired voice, "Young man, my name is Adam Samuels. I'm a veteran and I'd appreciate your help in taking Old Glory down. Will you help me, young man?"

EPILOGUE

The Cirrus, literally flooded with storm waters, went down in the Cape May marshes just off the Golden State Parkway. When Sunny pulled the CAPS lever in the Cirrus, a solid-fuel rocket blew out the top hatch of the aircraft. This deployed the Cirrus Airframe Parachute System. The aircraft and occupants, although wet, tired and black and blue, suffered only the equivalent of a ten- to twelve-foot jump off a building as the Cirrus struts and seats absorbed the impact of the ballistic chute touch-down.

Actually, according to the FAA, the impact was made even less by the fact that the craft and passengers deployed over and landed in the thick Cape May marshes.

Sunny and Wolfe lived to fly again another day.

The Shark and two of her attractive young administrative assistants were held for trial in relation to the Hughes Center bombings.

Trog Svladen, a foreign national, is awaiting trial for the murder of a young banner-towing pilot from Wildwood Crest. He is also awaiting charges for the death of a Carnegie Mellon professor in the Strip District of Pittsburgh, Pennsylvania.

The Tomcat pilot and RIO were questioned about the targeting of the Jet Ranger helicopter. It was determined they were following orders and that, under the circumstances, it was an unfortunate "friendly fire" accident.

Matt and Shepherd stayed on at the Hughes Center. Wolfe visits Cape May and mooches off his friends frequently.

Matt and Sunny are together. Sunny is giving Matt flying lessons in the restored Cirrus. Matt is given special leave and disappears for weeks at a time from his Hughes Center job. Sunny takes too many vacations from her English teaching position. Shepherd and Wolfe know where they go. But they aren't talking.

There is a second memorial at Sunset Beach, just to the north of the Cement Ship. The remains of the tail section of a Jet Ranger helicopter juts out from the Atlantic for all to see. On the tail there are the names and ranks of the veterans who died in Big Cheese. In one of the tourist areas at the checkout counter beside the seashells, there is a laminated sheet of paper, free for the asking. It tells the story of the Cement Ship and the Jet Ranger. All that is said about the ship is true. Some of the truth about Wink, Spiffy and Poor Man is also there.

THE END

Printed in the United States
49725LVS00006B/118

Dither Me Dead

Pilot Sunny Patronski doesn't want to begin her day flying to a forensics lab, especially since her only passenger is a corpse in a crime scene recovery bag. Sunny is drawn into the maelstrom when plastination (contemporary mummification art) [illegible] it man cross her path. She and Matt Harmond, h[illegible] friend, become targets of the madman. Togethe[illegible] rtrum Randolph, an amoral techno-terrorist entrepreneur with a GPS dithering device that turns terrorism into a profitable business. Sunny and Matt team up with Wolfe, a retired FBI agent, and Pat Shepherd, ex-Special Forces director of security at the William J. Hughes Technical Center near Atlantic City, New Jersey. *Dither Me Dead* is fiction but the catastrophic possibilities are real.

Jim Opalka was born in Pennsylvania in 1944. He received a B.A. from Grove City College and an M.S. from Slippery Rock University. He is a certified flight instructor and holds commercial and advanced ground instructor ratings. He has written numerous articles in aviation and related magazines. He lives with his wife, Paula, in Butler, Pennsylvania. Visit *www.jameswopalka.com* for further information.

Cover art by Corey and Bill Daum

ISBN 1-4137-9871-3

90000

9 781413 798715

Publish America

www.PublishAmerica.com